I0639677

All Gods Children

Alex Mitchell

Published by Alex Mitchell, 2024.

This is a work of fiction. Similarities to real people, places, or events are entirely coincidental.

ALL GODS CHILDREN

First edition. January 8, 2024.

Copyright © 2024 Alex Mitchell.

ISBN: 979-8891980235

Written by Alex Mitchell.

Also by Alex Mitchell

Welcome to Shepherds Pass
Revenge at Shepherds Pass
Treasure at Shepherds Pass
Welcome to Shepherds Pass
Man Among the Missing
Noreen Tyler
Robinhood at Shepherds Pass
That Which Makes Us Who We Are
Secrets That Bind Family
Balance of Power in Shepherds Pass
All Gods Children

I dedicate this book to my late son, Almo. May you forever rest in peace in our hearts. I also dedicate this to my daughter Carla who has through adversity been made a brave, proud and strong woman.

Chapter 1

"Do you have a name for your fish?" Nicky sat in the comfortable overstuffed recliner in the Physiatrist office, watching the fish swim in the large tank.

"Yes, as a matter of fact, I do. Now, let me ask you a question." Doctor Beverly Shane walked from behind her large Oak desk. She sat in a chair facing Nicky. Doctor Shane was one of those women who, even no longer in her youth, saw no need to surrender to the standard views on sex and aging. She wore a sleek business suit that conformed to her figure. She sat and crossed her long, thin legs as she began writing on a notepad in her lap. "When was the last time you killed someone?"

Nicholas Braden, or Nicky as he had become know is a private investigator for the law firm of Woodbridge Foster and Klein. Their client list includes trust fund babies, movie stars and gangsters. Nicky and his twin Nichole or Cole as she preferred to be called often worked together. It was not uncommon for the toughest of cases, and cases that might require the law to be broken to be assigned to the Braden twins.

Nicky kept watching the fish. "I am not sure."

"Nicky, I am a doctor, so doctor-patient privilege applies. You are a private investigator for a law firm, so anything not covered under one set of privileges certainly is covered by the other." She sat back in her chair, content to let Nicky weigh her comments. Covertly she hoped he noticed her legs. Dr Shane was assigned to annually evaluate any agent in the field who carried a gun. She took her job seriously. She knew that Nicky suffered from some form of mental issues that may be psychopathological or socio-psychological, but he functioned. She felt that research on him could help many people if he would allow it. Her questions were drawn out of a concern that he sometimes lost control in dangerous rages to solve violent issues. Then later returned to normal or as close to the norm as to fit in with everyday people.

Nicky stopped looking at the fish and took at the green eyes of Dr Shane. "I assure you I am not evading your question. And I was not in some form of blackout."

Dr. Shane adjusts herself in her chair, leaning forward to take advantage of Nicky's desire to help her understand.

"The guy I shot last. Well, I am not sure I killed him."

"How many times did you shoot him?"

"Seven or eight."

A mix of shock and horror overtook the Doctor's face, but she quickly recovered. "What makes you think you might not have killed him?"

"The woman with me shot him just as many times, and it is hard to know which bullet did the deed."

Dr Shane wrote for a moment, not looking up at Nicky.

"I shot a guy in the neck the day before. The guy was trying to crush the car I was in with a bulldozer. If that helps for an answer. Sure, I killed him. Thank God."

"Do you ever feel remorse?" She asked.

"Probably less than the fish would for doing what it had to do survive."

The Doctor held her pad down and stared at Nicky. "Please do make fun. I know you believe in the process and have made great progress."

Nicky began watching the fish again.

"When you were a child, were you and your twin sister close?"

"Yes."

"How close?"

"Very close we still are. We help each other."

"When you were young children, did the two of you ever have any accidental or exploratory sexual contact? Before you answer, I want you to know it is not shameful or vulgar. "Nicky stood up and walked to the fish tank, picked up the fish food, and sprinkled a little into the tank, watching the fish surround the falling food.

"No. Never."

"Did you break up with Vivian?"

"Yes."

"Why?"

"She was taking control, and it was choking the life out of any chance for a long-term relationship."

Doctor Shane was now writing feverishly. "So, the fact that she is older that you didn't matter?"

"No. My current girlfriend, Connie, is the same age as her."

"Why do you think you gravitate toward older women?" Dr. Shane asked, resting her pen on her lips. A pose that did not tell if it was for clinical research or her personal interest.

"I don't know, but I look for a particular emotional security, and if it is not there or is violated, then all is lost.

Nicky and Dr Shane talked a little more, but he knew she would clear his gun permit for the future. He wanted to help with whatever she was researching if it did not involve physical testing. It is a common belief in the psychological profession that the difference between a psychopath and a sociopath is that the psychopath is born, but the social path is made. Nicky felt that whatever the mental issue he and his sister shared, it ran through both, and the shared love between them kept the monsters of their mental disarray at bay.

Chapter 2

Nicole stepped out of the fire engine red convertible Corvette wearing stiletto high heels and a red mini skirt with a gold zipper up the front. She wore a black see-through blouse that displayed her pink laced bra. Nicole, a brunette, wore a big, curly blonde wig and large gold earrings matching the bracelets and bangles on her wrists. She switched across the parking lot of the Redstone Bar in Clovis, California. There was a country cover band poorly playing some popular country tunes and mangling them as best they could. A large policeman stood resting against his car near the entrance. "Well, do you have a big gun officer?" Nicole commented, looking at the policeman's belt buckle. "Your first target is in the back wearing a red baseball cap. Good hunting." He commented in a cold, impersonal tone. Inside was some Californian's wet dream of what a down-home bar should look like, complete the straw on the floors.

"Hey, sweetheart, I know I haven't seen you here before. It must be my lucky night." A big barrel-chested guy with a poorly groomed beard and plaid shirt approached Nicole.

"Well, it might be only I got a date tonight. But I might be meeting a girlfriend here later. Are you going to be around for a while? She is wild, and a big guy like yourself might be just a ticket to get her to the top of the mountain. If you know what I mean." Nicole winked.

"I'll be in the back at the pool tables if you need me; my name is Buck."

Nicole squeezed her way through the crowd of drunken revelers doing their impersonations of dancing. She located the guy in the red cap. Nicole sat down on the stool next to him. The bartender and an older man with a grey beard and a sixties bicker look appeared. "What can I get you, honey?"

"Beer anything cold and in a bottle and a refill for him." Nicole began fishing in her oversized arm bag.

"Look, I can buy my own drink. And don't waste your time. I can't afford your price." The guy is the cap, informed Cole.

"Oh my god, a girl tries to buy a guy a drink, and he calls her a whore." Nicole screamed, then turned to the bartender. "What kind of place is this? If my brother were here, he would ask you to step outside for that comment. I work in the insurance office. I try to buy a guy a drink, and he insults me."

"Calm down, lady." Red Cap tried to touch Nichol's arm, and she pulled it away.

"Look honey, my name is Pete, and I don't know what gets into these young, pretty boys sometimes. In my day, if a girl wanted to start a conversation with me, I wouldn't fag out on them." the bartender explained.

"There is a guy named Buck in the pool room. Could you send him a drink on me." Nicole asked Pete.

"Okay, hold on, I apologize." Red cap stated. Nicole smiled. "Pete, give them both a drink on me." And handed Pete a fifty-dollar bill.

"Behave yourself, Chance. This girl is only trying to make friends.

Can't you see she isn't from around here?" Pete offered, and he returned with the drinks. "They call me Chance. How do you know Buck?"

"I don't. He asked me to leave with him if things didn't work out with you." She smiled and sipped her beer.

"AFTER YOU." CHANCE offered, opening the door to his double-wide trailer home for Nicole.

"No, the lights are off, and if I trip over these heels, no orgasm for either of us tonight."

Cole had driven Chance to his trailer following a brief conversation riddled with lies on her part.

Chance walked into the room and immediately felt a huge electric shock. All his nerves fired at once, and he convulsed violently on the floor. Nicole stood over him, smiling. "You know this is a new stun gun, and I keep forgetting to turn it down." She rolled him over, handcuffed him, and duct-taped his legs. Nicole pulled him further into the room and pulled a syringe out of her purse. "This is to keep you from wandering off. You will notice I am not sterilizing the needle." She pulled down the back of his jeans and jabbed an injection into his hip. She duct-taped his mouth. "We will have so much fun when I get back."

The police car was parked outside with the same policeman Nicole had seen before sitting in the car. "Second target is just about to get off work. Go do your thing."

"Hey Lowell," Nicole called out as the tall, thin man in overalls walked from the service station, cleaning his hands on a shop towel.

"Do we know each other, pretty lady?"

Nicole switched closer to Lowell and leaned against him. "We are supposed to be getting together at Chance's trailer. A friend is waiting with him, but I want to ask you something." Nicole stepped back and eyed Lowell, looking him up and down. "Anything, pretty lady."

"Well, I know I am supposed to do the thing with Chance and you with her, but how do you feel about a little four-way switch up at some point?"

"Would you like for me to drive?" Were the next coherent words out of Lowell's mouth?

LOWELL DROPPED ON THE floor after his stun, even harder than Chance. "Damn thing, that must have been up, not down." After securing Lowell, Nicole slid the two men together and ripped off the tape from Chance's mouth. She removed a small torch from her bag and lit it. Both men's eyes bulged. Nicole straddled Chance's legs as he sat on the floor with his bound hands behind his back. "First, we talk." Chance and Lowell looked too terrified to speak. "A brother is supposed to protect his sister. To love her and to be there for her even if the relationship between them and their parents fails." There was a slight tear in the corner of Nicole's eye. Cole slowly ran the fingers from her free hand through the oily mess that Chance considered his hair. "You failed to do this now, Libby is a thing more like me than she should be."

"Libby, that dike sister of mine put you up to this." Chance spat out at her.

"No, you put me up to it. See, you wanted her to be like me. Now, here is the real me." And she placed the flame of the torch on his chest. There was the smell of burning hair and flesh, followed by the smell of burning bone. He screamed and cried, then broke wind and began choking on his own saliva. Chance passed out from shock and pain. Nicole got off Chance and began pulling down Leo's pants. "Let's see what we have here."

"Please, lady, don't do this. I am sorry." Lowell cried out just before she put the torch to his testicles. Both men seem to have passed out from the massive pain or the siren song of death as Nicole undressed, put her clothes in a plastic bag, and slipped on a jumpsuit. As a departing gift, Nicole pulled the pin on an A7 incendiary grenade, and the trailer was in full blaze in seconds.

"How long should I let it burn before I call it in." The policeman had pulled up beside Nicole, watching the trailer burn.

"I think they are about done."

"Tell Marlstone it's over. My debt is now paid." The patrolman informed Cole with guilt, lacing his comment. Marlstone was the local controlling gangster, and the officer owed him a favor. Cole was obligated to check in with the local crime family if she would be operating on their turf. This would prevent any conflicts of interest that might occur.

"Marlstone knows that." She reached into the car, pulled an envelope filled with cash from beneath the seat of the Corvette, and threw it into the police car."

"What the hell is that for."

"A gift from me personally. This meant a lot to me. I hate rapists. Especially the ones that would rape a child."

The sports car made its howl as it vanished into the night. The deed was done.

"WHY ARE YOU STILL IN California, young lady?" Inez was the coordinator for much of the law firm that Cole worked for.

"Finishing up some personal business." Nicole had answered the phone in the car as she sped to the private airfield.

"Don't get smart with me, young lady. You aren't too grown for me to put you over my lap."

"Sorry, Inez."

"I want all of your rosy cheeks on that plane and in Shane's office first thing in the morning."

"Yes, ma'am."

"And keep it under 80. I show you nearing 100 miles an hour on the satellite."

Chapter 3

"**Y**ou must be Miss Holley." The small girl in a business suit guessed. She wore her hair in a resemblance to the way Nicole and Nicky wore their hair; only her hair was blonde, not brown like the Braden's. She had a double ear piercing and dark eye shadow. She stood in the doorway of the Braden home facing the Woman in her sixties with eyes that matched Nicholas and Nicole's deep double brown eyes.

"You must be Libby; the twins have told me so much about you. Turn around." Unclear as to why Libby did a turn.

"Nicky said you had a great tight butt." Libby blushed and looked at a total loss for a remark.

"Where is Cole? She said she needed me here?"

"Libby, there must be a mistake. Cole is in New York. Up for an annual psychological review."

Libby looked confused. "Well, I guess I can wait at the hotel until I contact her."

"No way. There is no way you are in town, and you are leaving me alone in this house by myself while you are alone in a room across town. Bring yourself in here, and you can help me pack up this old place. Nicky has built a new house, and they want my old bones to tag along for some reason."

"That sounds great, Miss Holley."

"Wrong, it's Aunt Holley to you, little lady. Now let me get you something to eat, and I will show you around."

Chapter 4

"When you and your brother were in your treehouse, did he ever touch you in any special way?" Dr. Shane asked Nicole.

"What kind of freak are you," Cole screamed at the Doctor.

"Nicole, the degree of your protest tells a lot about how true your answer is. Nicole stood up walked over to Doctor Shane's desk and slapped the cup of hot coffee that sat in from of her, splashing hot coffee all over Dr Shane. Cole grabbed the Doctor by the throat and pushed her back, smacking her head against the wall behind her.

"If you ever say something like that about my brother and me, I am going to choke you to death." Nicole stopped choking the Doctor just prior to Dr Shane passing out. The receptionist heard the commotion and ran into the room just in time for Cole to bump her hard leaving the room. The receptionist ran to the Doctor, who was now coughing and struggling to regain her breath.

"Don't ever let that physio near me again." The receptionist looked at Shane. "Then you want to fail her application to carry a weapon?"

"Hell no. Do you think I want her back in here really pissed off? Pass the bitch with flying colors."

Chapter 5

"Adam." the whispered voice on the phone tried to confirm. "Yes, why are you calling this late at night?"

"Who are you whispering to so late at night." Adam's wife asked. She was not used to Adam taking calls on his private home number at night. Adam is the head partner for Woodbridge Foster and Klein, Nicky and Coles boss. Adam and his wife were awaken by the phone ring.

"Tell Nicky I don't blame him if I don't make it. It was all my fault you told him to stop being my friend."

"It's sister Amanda," Adam informed his wife.

"You mean the little one with the hots for Nicky Braden?"

"What's wrong, sister?" Adam asked.

"He must help. It's not about me; my flesh has been a sacrifice. It's about all God's children."

There was a crashing sound that Adam could make out, followed by what sounded like a gunshot. Then the line went dead.

"Dear, it would appear that I made a major miscalculation."

"You will fix it. You always do. Now get some sleep."

Chapter 6

"**I**s there anything I can get for you or your wife to make you a little more confrontable, Mr. Brown?" Mr. and Mrs. Brown sat in the offices of Barr and Fleishman. The Bar and Fleishman office was a doctor's office but did not resemble many standard Doctor's offices. It looked more like the office of an international investment firm.

Mrs. Brown cried uncountably as her husband tried to communicate for both. "We don't need anything but our son to be well."

"I certainly can understand that." Cecil Barr sympathized.

"The doctors are telling us to prepare for our son to die. He needs a transplant, but there are no special considerations in the way the networks work." Mr. Brown ranted.

"Please, there must be something someone can do. Whatever the cost." Mrs. Brown called out from her weeping. This was the magic word, Donavan, Cecil's twin brother, had been waiting to hear.

"Folks, my brother is an excellent surgeon with excellent resources for support staff. But we had an issue." Donavan now saw his opening.

"Move it, conquer it, or just plain destroy the obstacle. That's how I built my empire." Mr. Brown stated, hugging his wife closely.

"Let's outline where we are, shall we? The transplant networks are set up to give equal consideration and opportunity to all who need the organs. It is notable at face value, but let's consider the real world. Let's say there are future rapist and gang bangers in line in front of your son.

Is it fair that their lives should be saved so they will kill or rape one day? Now take your son, who, if allowed to live, might become the president of the greatest nation on earth someday."

"Oh god, my thoughts exactly. There must be something someone can do." Mr. Brown questioned.

"Let's say we can get the organ and implant it. Guarantee that if it is rejected, we have a standby waiting for a replacement. We get the blood and all the medical items taken care of. We do this for a fee that may be more than some others would ask, but we provide the one thing they don't, and that is a guarantee to act the moment you shake my hand." Cecil explained.

"You could do that?" Mrs. Brown look a little relieved.

"Yes, but we need to clear up a few things. First, you cannot discuss our agreement with any law enforcement agencies. We are stepping outside the law to save your child." Donavan interjected.

"That sounds fair. Medicine bogged down by law is a death sentence to Jonathan." Mr. Brown commented.

"Next, our fees may be high, so we will give you options to pay us that won't destitute you. If you have securities that need to be cashed in, we can wait for a maturity day or a higher point of return." Donavan explained.

"You see, my brother's strong suit is business. So many in my profession do not understand economics and would take your last nickel." Cecil smiled. "And we realize we are not responsible for all God's children."

"Write it up, and we will sign." Mr. Brown stated that his wife's face showed something it had not in months. Hope.

Chapter 8

Still angry over the encounter with Dr Shane and wondering how she would explain it to Nicky when she had promised to behave. Cole turned the corner to run to the elevator and crashed into a young man about her age. It caused the papers he carried to flip out and hit the floor. "Lousy stupid freak." She grunted.

"I am sorry, Miss Cole." The young man commented quickly.

"Not you, that Doctor. She says nasty things to get a reaction then..." Cole froze and noticed the guy was staring at her face as if being this close to her was a lifelong dream. It made her blush and feel special. "You know who I am?"

"You are like a legend."

"Don't say that it's flattering, but I just work around here."

"My name is Matt. I work in the Nest." The Nest was the nickname for computer operations and research for the law firm and accounting. "Can we go across the street for lunch? I am still pissed off. I don't know what to tell my brother."

"I have work."

"I can clear it. Inez is a friend of mine."

With the subtle tone that came from an unplanned first date, Cole made the arrangement, and they ventured forward to learn about each other. This date would be the first of many as they began building an implied trust that, at some point, would need to be expressly defined.

Chapter 9

"Mrs. Harris, the people of my congregation are outraged over your plan to move them out of their homes and replace the current housing with luxury developments that only yuppies can afford. We won't stand for it." Reverend Mead bellowed out in a preaching tone. His wife, the First Lady Mead, stood by his side, nodding in total agreement. Reverend Mead was a portly black man with a handsome face greying around the temples. The Meads had come to the office of Connie Harris in New York. Connie Harris was the owner operator of Harris Development. Harris Development was developing housing for plants being opened or reopened to bring jobs back to the US. The principal investors in Harris Development were mostly the children, grandchildren, and great-grandchildren of Gangsters who had legitimate money to invest. Large investment houses had turned many children with a tainted legacy away because of the sins of their forefathers.

"Reverend, I think there has been a misunderstanding," Connie offered. Mavis, Connie's assistant, a black woman of UK descent, entered the room pushing a small serving cart with cookies and coffee.

"I thought some refreshments might be in order." Mavis tried to hide her British accent in that it sometimes alienated her from American blacks, but the accent still reared its head.

"And where are you from, young lady." The first lady asked.

"California, by way of Westchester, ma'am."

Connie thought it a good time to steer the conversation back on course. "The housing being constructed is for the factory that is being built in your neighborhood. Good jobs, and you won't have to commute or travel to the ends of the earth for decent schools and housing."

"Tell me more." The reverend asked, shoveling cookies in his mouth. "Private investors feel we are sending away too much opportunity out of this country. Crime is up. The country we love is falling apart on our watch. We need to reevaluate what we can do from the standpoint of private business instead of waiting for the government to realize the severity of our problems. Too often, they make promises and shake hands, but their actions tell a different tail. I am hoping for people such as yourself to help provide the moral leadership that leads young families into productive lives."

"So, you are saying it's not a land grab?"

"No, quite the opposite," Mavis added.

"Where do you go to church, young lady?' the first lady asked Mavis.

"My home church is in California. I have been trying to find one when I work here, but most of what I see is too big and impersonal. Don't get me wrong, I love business, but it's not what I need when I pray. Also, my husband and children are not here, so I am skeptical a woman alone without people to introduce her in the local churches."

The first lady's eyes looked as if they were going to explode. "We can give you a card to check out our church." Connie reached out to touch Mavis, and it was as if she misjudged the distance. Connie fainted.

"GOD, I RUINED THE MEETING," Connie told Maxine as she realized where she was. Connie was in a hospital room. A young girl in scrubs came in, reading a chart at the foot of the bed.

"Is she going to be alright," Mavis asked.

"Well, I am not the Doctor; I am a dietitian. She needs to watch the diet and get plenty of rest, at least until the baby is born."

"Baby." Mavis and Connie screamed at the same time.

"Gee, did I let the cat out of the bag? Usually, when a woman your age gets pregnant, it's from trying."

"Mavis, get Nicky."

"I called his office, and he and Cole are both in the field."

"Get that damn Nicolas Braden. I don't care what you have to do."

Chapter 10

"Get in the car, Braden." Agent Sharon Winchester demanded. She was an FBI Special Agent and had a course relationship with Nicolas and Nicole Braden. She did not like that they operated with impunity on certain matters, and the law handcuffed her.

"I'm working, but I appreciate the offer," Nicky responded. Sharon had caught Nicky headed to his car from a meeting at the Law firm where he works.

"Get in the fucking car, or I swear I will pop a cap in your ass and plant a gang banger piece on the ground."

Nicky got in the car. She drove for a moment, then pulled over. "Are you packing?" Sharon asked.

"No, I am on my way to the church on Eighteenth Street, and they hate guns."

"Don't mind if I don't take your word, do you?" Sharon began running her hands over Nicky. "You know, years ago, I was a rookie cop in DC. I rode with a lot of screwed-up cops. Some would pull over in the projects, put a young black girl in the car, and feel her up. Kind of like I am doing to you." Nicky showed no change in expression while she slowly ran her hand wherever she wanted. "One day, one pitifully sick old cop I was working with pulled some old black grandmother over and massaged her crotch while her husband and son stood there helpless to stop it. At that point, I knew it had nothing to do with sex." Sharon stopped with her hand on Nicky's crotch. "I was all about showing the enemy you had all power and could do anything you please."

"Agent Winchester, you are angry with me. Why don't you drive me to the meeting at the Church, and we can discuss it."

"Civil, aren't we." She stopped touching him, put the car in drive, and was off. "I got a big problem, and I think you are at the root of it."

"I see."

"No, you semi-psychotic son of a bitch, you don't, but you will if you don't fix what you started."

Sharon Winchester was a stocky woman of less-than-beautiful features. She looked like a women's correctional officer with the stern expression she projected.

"I can't fix the problem if you don't tell me what it is." Nicky reasoned.

"Well, let's see. Agent McLaughlin gets promoted to assistant director. He is a trust fund baby climbing the latter for political reasons and needs more street sense to fill a thimble. The shot at the second assistant director's job should be mine."

"Congratulations."

"Fuck you."

"We are headed to a church, so you might want to level out of some of the cursing," Nicky recommended.

"Maddox, that lecherous fossil. We found him wasting away at Interpol and were going to let him cruise to retirement. Now it turns out he is busting down doors solving past gangland murders and arresting crooked cops that are part of a national murder-for-hire network."

Nicky kept staring straight ahead, unsure how much she knew of his involvement with the makeover of Agent Maddox.

"A little birdie told me that his massive transformation came after a chat with you in the backroom of a hospital in California."

"You should not believe everything birdies tell you."

"Just tell me, Braden, what did he do to get your help? Tell me he sucked your dick. At least I can understand. If you help me, I'll do it right here and now." They had pulled up to the parking for the Church.

"I'm fairly sure doing that here, the Church would frown on that."

Winchester was giving Nicky a mean stare when his cell phone rang.

"Hey, Smokie."

"You bringing my money by today? Amanda told me you were out of town." Smoke asked.

Nicky had no idea why Amanda had used Smokie's illegal services. Nicky got a call for Inez to meet with his boss Adam. Adam was afraid for Sister Amanda. Adam had received a call that made him feel Amanda's life was in jeopardy. Amanda and Nicky had been close friends working on charities together. Sister Sophia felt that the close friendship between Amanda and a man like Nicky was improper and had complained to Adam. Adam had asked Nicky to no longer have contact with Amanda for her best interest.

"How much do I owe you?" Nicky asked.

"Four and a half. I gave her a discount. Usually, it's six for two."

"I'll bring the six by later today. You got to eat too."

"Always the class act. You and your sister. By the way, you want to bring enough cash for Richie. He called that day Amanda stopped by to verify it was cool to put a charge on your credit."

Nicky's mind started racing. The relationship between Amanda and himself was not what Sister Sophia suspected. It was that Amanda was addicted to detective novels. She read and watched anything on Private Detectives. The private detectives she loved most weren't real. Being a Private Detective himself, he knew that and tried to keep her from romanticizing. He had even enlisted her help on occasion to let her get a feel for what was real until the night that he had rescued the Assistant District Attorney's wife and daughter. The District Attorney's wife and daughter had been gang-raped, and he had no reference for how to comfort them. Amanda had worked wonders. Anamda had done for him the things he could not do himself and felt in her debt. Wherever she was whatever she need he would try to resolve the issue.

"WELL, NICOLAS BRADEN, did you come to abscond with another of my young charges."

Nicolas had been led into the office of Sister Sophia by Sister Margret, a young nun with a major overbite and heavy-looking glasses. Sister Margret looked at Nicky like men were more mythical creatures than unicorns.

"Perhaps you can plan a romantic weekend with Sister Margret," Sophia commented. "What do you say, Sister Margret? You up for some slap and tickle."

"I am here because Adam got a disturbing call from Amanda, and he thinks she is in trouble. Personally, if I must stand here and let you attack me, then bring it on."

"I thought she left with you."

"No. Adam wanted me to distance myself from her for a while. He sent me on a job in California."

Sister Sophia sat back in an old velvet chair behind her antique desk. The office had pictures of Cardinals and Popes of the past.

"I see you as the ignominious merchant of death, Mr. Braden."

"If she dies and you could have helped me stop it, then you would have been the one who dealt out her death. And you would have done it to spite me. I am not worth it; please find a different day to slaughter me. Help her. I am begging you."

Nicholas nor Sophia seemed to pay any attention to the fact that Margaret was still standing there until she gasped at Nicky's statement. Sophia raised and walked to Margert. "Sister, I want you to assist Mr. Braden. Show him Sister Amanda's cell and answer any questions you might be able to. Now, both of you leave my office. I have work to do."

"DO WOMEN REALLY THROW themselves at you?" Sister Margret asked Nicky when they were alone in Sister Amanda's cell. Sister Margaret had insisted on leaving the door wide open for fear some might think they were seeking a place to do something inappropriate. Sister Amanda's cell had all the homeliness of a prison cell. There was a bed that looked more like an army cot and a disturbing lack of personal attachments to her life. What was there was books. Piles of books all on detective stories past and present. Nicky noticed there was a map of the UN lying on top of a small dresser.

"Amanda reads anything detective related. My favorites are romance novels. I must admit I am a junkie for them." Nicky smiled at Margaret's confession. "Might I ask you a question? For research purposes." Margret asked.

"Sure."

"Do you really have sex with a lot of different women?"

"No."

"But you get a lot of offers." Nicky continued to search for anything that might be out of place. He noticed a parking stub. Why would someone who did not have a car have a city parking stub?

"I have a girlfriend. I am hoping to marry her. She is busy building a business, and I am building two houses in different places because the business operates off both coasts. I prefer living in the Midwest whenever I can. As soon as things calm down, I want to walk her down the aisle."

"You sound so normal to be so hated by the Mother Superior." Nicky smiled again. "Amanda did not have a car, but do you know if she could drive?"

"Yes, but poorly, just between us."

"I KEPT TRYING TO DRIVE away and leave your butt here, but curiosity got the better of me." Agent Winchester was waiting with her car at the curb when Nicky had concluded his search of the cell.

"Missing Nun."

"Missing like kidnapped or Missing like most likely dead?"

"US Bank, please, and how big are your hands in relationship to those of normal women."

"WELL, CUZ I KNEW EVEN if we live in a world where a nun would rip you off, Nicky and Cole Braden won't," Smokie affirmed his theory of life. Nicky stood in a small donut shop that Smokie owned. Smokie is the supplier of the best fake IDs in New York. He was called Smokie because of his resemblance to a young Smokie Robinson. The shop did a brisk business, keeping the people coming for fake ID unnoticeable.

"Why is the ugly woman driving you around?"

"She is with the FBI."

"You are turning her out, or is she just the best head on the planet, and that mug doesn't matter?"

"I am trying to find someone and might need her help. Let me see the pictures."

Smokie showed a look of indignation. "What pictures."

"Smokie, anytime anybody has fake IDs made and doesn't pay cash, you keep a copy of the info in your computer. That way, you can send a collector, and the guy you send knows the fake name and face."

"Oh, those pictures. I keep forgetting you are more gangster than my regular clientele."

Smokie returned with a picture of Sister Amanda and, the name fake name Freda Payne and the picture of a black woman Nicky did not recognize. The name of the photo read Shirley Brown. "Cool, huh."

"What is it with you and old-school music?"

"Well, your friend, the black chick best keeps her mouth shut."

"Why is that."

"African accent. Don't sound like no soul singer I ever heard Motown put out."

"LEOS JEWELRY," NICKY instructed, returning to Sharon in the car.

"Explain again why I am chauffeuring you around."

"Because I am working a case, and you want in if possible. We both know that you will follow me wherever I go until you find out if there is a piece you can claim for your own."

"Smart ass."

"Call it the price of feeling me up. I came cheap, so to speak."

"SWEETHEART, I HAVE to ask you a favor," Cole answered the phone. The caller ID told her it was Inez. Cole was concerned that the coffee incident with the Doctor the other day would cause a problem. She knew her best option was to let Inez speak so she could locate the points to defend her actions.

"Anything Miss Inez."

"Digger is in town, and he got here before I could decide on a place to put him, so do you mind him camping on the couch in the place I got for you until the place for him is ready?"

"No problem. Did you hear anything from Dr. Shane?"

"Yes, you passed with flying colors. She says she doesn't want to see you again for at least a year."

"What about my brother."

"He passed, too."

"Digger is a little afraid of me. Are you sure he wants to stay with me?"

"Just behave. By the way, I hear you have been borrowing Matt from the Nest. Is this personal or business?"

"I hope it's personal. I like him a lot."

"Good. You deserve some happiness, baby."

Chapter 11

"**M**r. Braden, we received the notice from your bank verifying the amounts you can be allowed to work with. I wish so many more of our clients had the foresight to have their banks clear them." Leo stood about five feet tall with a slight curve to his posture, making him look even shorter. He wore a white shirt and black pants, as did all the workers in the jewelry store. They also wore Yakamas.

"Is this the lucky lady?' Leo asked, staring in disbelief at Agent Winchester and not showing his shock.

"No, she's my hand model."

"She has large knuckles for a hand model."

"Fuck you, shorty," Winchester responded.

"Maybe after we see some rings, you can show me some riding crops." Nicky joked.

"I don't carry them as a rule, but in this case, I would be happy to send them out." Leo led them to the back room to view the more impressive items.

HOLLY WAS AMAZED AS he reached the bottom of the steps to the basement in the Missouri home of the Braden's. She stood watching Libby, admiring herself in a long cream-colored dress. Holley had made the dress for Nicole but could not remember Cole ever wearing the dress. Now, the dress and many more like it had made their way to a box of future discards. It not only fit Libby, who is smaller in frame than Cole, but it accentuated her features. Libby's face also registered a look that told such a fine dress was not something she wore on a regular basis or had seldom owned in her life.

"Oh. I'm sorry. I saw you were getting rid of all these wonderful things, and I could not help myself." Libby stood embarrassed as much by my being caught trying on the dresses as indulging in vanity in general.

"I made those for Nicole. When I got the kids, they were teens, and Nicole mostly followed Nicky around dressed like him. At one point, I thought if I made pretty things for her, she would want to wear them, you know, appear more ladylike." Holley smiled. The memories were good, and with the twins gone so much, the more recent memories were not as plentiful. "She was your size when I made those."

"Oh, really. You made these?"

"Yes, my aunt taught me to sew. Her mother taught her, but I could not hand the tradition down." Holly searched through a box and found a form-fitting party dress. "Try this one on." Libby quickly shed the dress she was wearing and then turned to notice Holly staring at the tattoos on her body. 'Why do you mark yourself."

Libby sat down beside Holly. "I guess I should tell you I am bisexual, and this is part of how I identify myself."

"Bullshit." Libby looked shocked. "Can I tell you a secret? I was with women before you were born. There is no form of cheap advertising on yourself required. If you decide you want to mark yourself, do it because it's what you want, not because it advertises who you think you should be." It was the same motherly digging herself in that made Nicole so fond of Holley. "Yes, ma'am," Libby answered.

"Now try this one on."

RICKY WAS A CAR THIEF who stole cars and license plates and sold them to people, usually to people who wanted a car to commit a crime and needed the car to be passable on the streets for a few hours a day. Sister Amanda and gotten a beat-up Ford from Ricky and Nicky had paid her bill. The only problem now was where was she headed. Nicky remembered the UN pamphlet in Amanda's cell and directed Winchester to drive toward the UN. Just before reaching the UN, Nicky noticed the city parking matched the stub he had seen, and there was a hotel next to the lot.

Chapter 12

"Look, the manager is going to call the cops."

A freckled face girl threatened the six large black men in suits who were at the check-in desk.

"I don't care if he calls his mother. You are going to assist are you are creating an international incident."

Winchester and Nicky stared at each other on hearing the man's African accent.

"Bingo," Winchester stated.

"Ma'am, we are looking for someone who might be in trouble." Nicky pushed past the largest to the Black men at the desk.

"Look at his picture." Nicky showed her the picture of the Woman calling herself Shirly Brown, making sure the black men in suits saw the picture.

"This is Doctor Ottumwa. Why do you have this picture." The lead Blackman yelled.

"I think she is with a friend of mine, and they may be in trouble."

"I am Bah of the United National Guard. The Doctor is missing, and these people refuse to help."

"Look, sir, I will tell you just as I told them. We don't give out room numbers to anyone." Freckles repeated.

"Right now, your manager is in the back, hiding under his desk. He is leaving you to deal with a pro football team front line by yourself, hoping the police show up before the ball snaps. Bitch, wake up, you are on your own in this lobby. I tell you what. I am FBI agent Winchester on my authority; take us to their room or I will bag and tag your funny face ass." This brought a round of cheers from the guard.

"HOW BAD IS THIS MESS and, why is he here?" Agent Sheldon, Winchester's field supervisor, asked upon arrival. The room did not have Sister Amanda or Doctor Ottumwa, but there was blood and evidence of a struggle. Winchester declared it a crime scene and called for the local police to assist. She then contacted her supervisor, Tony Sheldon.

"He was working a case that parallels what our interest and to go around him would mean, losing time and possible evidence," Winchester answered in a tone that clearly let her supervisor know she knew more than he.

"What's our interest, and who is he working for?" Sheldon was not happy that his reference to Nicky being on the scene had gone answered.

"Well, sir, he is working for the Catholic Church; they have a missing nun. We have a missing foreign dignitary that was swiped on US soil and on our watch I might add."

Shelton looked like he had been hit with a stun gun. "Can you fix this? Do we need to push the panic button?"

"We need to find out the committees she was working on and what she was most passionate about. Somewhere in there is where she crosses paths with Sister Amanda." Nicky answered even though he knew he was not the one being asked.

"HURRY UP AND GET YOUR junk together and get it out of here. I got a guy coming over," Cole screamed to Digger. Digger and Cole had worked together on a job in California. Digger was a long-haired guy with a narrow face and eyes too close together. Cole had allowed him to sleep on the sofa now his room was ready, and she did now want to talk to Matt about Digger or the specifics of what she did for the law firm. Cole was also concerned that the relationship with Matt was going well and did not want to set off any jealous feelings before having the chance to explain that she worked with a lot of guys. Still, there was no physical relationship with any of them. Nicole returned to the bedroom to change the blouse she was thinking of wearing for her date for the fifth time. There was a knock at the door. Digger opened the door, still buttoning up his shirt. Matt stood there transfixed for a moment. Cole walked out of the bedroom, buttoning her blouse. In an instant, Matt was gone. "You got to go find him and explain," Digger told Cole.

"Why, maybe it wasn't meant to be."

"Then tell him that. What I saw on his face was that he was broken. I have been in his place before. The only person that can help him is you."

"Damn, you are right. I am going after him. Be sure you and your junk are out of here when we return."

Cole found Matt sitting on the curb by his car in the indoor parking garage for the hotel. His head was in his hands, and he looked sad and defeated. He was in no shape to drive a car. Cole sat down next to him.

"We need to talk."

"Who was I fooling? Someone like you interested in a guy from the tech department." Matt sounded like he was trying not to cry, but the emotion overwhelmed him quickly.

"Matt, please listen."

"No, you listen. All I got is who I am. I want to return to teaching, but it doesn't pay enough. I meet the only girl I have ever loved, and a guy is in line in front of me. God, I want to die."

"Stop that. You are right. Maybe I have been taking it slow, but it's only because I like to run things past my brother since we had a misunderstanding recently. I work with many guys just like a cop or fireman, but that doesn't mean I do anything with them."

They sat for a moment.

"Something ran through me when I felt I had hurt you. I felt a reflection of the sadness you felt. Please don't walk away now; let's go back to the room and share something other than hurt. Even if you feel you need to walk away, please don't walk away like this." Cole pleaded.

IN THE HOTEL ROOM, Cole had Matt sit on the sofa while she turned down the light. She went into the bedroom and returned wearing a kimono. She walked over to where he sat, then opened the kimono and was wearing only a red thong. She took his hand and placed them on her butt. "This is yours. Do with it as you please. From this point forward, we don't hurt each other anymore."

Chapter 13

"Nicky, I have been trying to contact you." Connie had finally been able to get Nicky.

"Is everything all right?"

"Well, that depends on how you look at all, alright. I fainted today."

"What."

"Well, the Doctor says I'll be fine. She says I must start eating better since I am pregnant."

There was a long silence on the phone.

"Nicky, are you still there."

"You know, it almost sounded like you said you are pregnant."

"I did."

"How."

"The usual way."

"Oh yeah, right."

"The doctor says that if we do not want it, we should let her know so she can do something as soon as possible."

"What does that mean?"

"It means the first time I go to kindergarten with our child, all the little kids are going to turn around and say, hey, there goes mother goose."

"Connie, I love you, but can we discuss this later face to face."

"Yes. I was so happy, then I started thinking, what if you did not feel the same way."

Connie hung up. This caused Nicky to call Holley and ask her to come to New York for assistance; he was happy that Libby was there with her but unsure why.

NICKY AND WINCHESTER sit around a large conference table. Finding the person, they need to assist them has taken a long time. Nicky used the time to refocus on his search, but events unfolding at home were trying to pop to the forefront of his thoughts.

"My name is Barbara. I am assistant to the Doctor."

"What was she working on that was so important." Winchester started.

"The missing children, of course."

"What missing children," Nicky asked.

"Some time back, a company bought out a couple of African orphanages that were filled with children from tribal warfare. The Dutch company moved the children, supposedly to a safer environment."

"So."

"So that environment must be in outer space because it is not on this planet." Barbara began passing documents that were dead ends to locate the whereabouts of the missing children.

Winchester and Nicky followed along in complete amazement. "I just got a cold shiver down my spine." Winchester comment.

"Welcome to the club. I have had the same chill for three months; that is when we connected Sister Amanda to track the donations end of it." Barbara Commented.

"I should have been there for her. This is way outside her depth." Nicky commented, not sure if it was her or Adam or Sister Sophia that should be sharing the guilt that was washing over him when he noticed a company he knew well—Lapone Refrigeration. This company did refrigerated transport owned by a mobster.

"I have got to call the CIA for help." Winchester looked at Nicky. "Don't worry I got to talk to some people who won't say a word around you."

A GROUP OF GUARDS LED Nicky and Cole into the dining room of the mansion in New Jersey. Nicky had decided for his sister to meet him drive with him to the house of the District Attorney Marcus Allison. The Allison home had all the warmth usually found in upper-middle-class homes.

The place was filled with pictures of the Allisons as a couple and of their daughter through various stages of their lives. There was nothing there that hinted at the terrible ordeal or abduction that that family had gone through. Allison is the DA who had been kidnapped with his family, his wife, and his daughter. The wife and daughter were gang raped while he has made to watch as torcher for his conviction of a drug lord. Because DA Allison had been pressuring and planning to take to trial a reputed mob boss named Costello when the abduction took place, all eyes went in his direction. Since the Roaring Twenties, there had been a long-standing unwritten agreement that police and federal authorities would not harass or confront members of a mob or suspected mob families that were not involved in criminal acts. The truce worked both ways. Mobsters, even some of the most violent, would never confront the family of police or federal authorities. The Costello incident threatened to redefine how confrontations between mob families and the authorities were approached. Costello spoke to Adam, his lawyer, who is also Nicky Braden's boss, and asked if he could do something to take the heat down before an eruption.

"I thought I might never see you again, Nicky. I guess I should refer to you as Mr. Braden, but I feel we have shared so much that I should be able to call you Nicky like everyone else does." A voice called to him from behind a doorway.

"Come on in here. There is someone I want you to meet." Amy came into the room and hugged Nicky.

"Amy, this is my sister Nicole; we call her Cole."

Amy walked over to Cole and stared. "She looks enough like you to be your twin."

"I am his twin."

Amy gave Cole a warm hug. Amy was a slender girl barely out of her teens who seemed to be recovering well physically but who knew about mental scaring. "It must be good to have a brother that understands how important it is to protect and remain close to his sister." Amy investigated Cole's face, waiting for a response.

"Brothers that don't understand that need to burn in hell or burn on their way to hell," Cole commented.

"It feels pretty good having her as a sister until she starts hiding things from me." Nicky admonished.

"I didn't hide anything from you. Things developed a little differently than I thought they would. Besides, I really like him and want you to meet him."

Amy stationed herself between the two of them. "Kind of nice to see you two argue; it's like nothing I have ever witnessed."

"I was wondering who could have brought my daughter out of hiding. I should have known it was Nicolas Braden." Mrs. Allison announced, stepping into the room.

"Wow, two of you. My husband is still on a call. Even though he is technically on leave, they still call him twenty times a day to ask for advice."

"Her name is Cole. She is his twin sister." Amy cleared it up.

"Amy, please take Cole on a tour of the house. I want to speak to Nicky alone for a moment before he sees your father." Mrs. Allison waited until Cole and Amy were clearly out of hearing range before speaking.

"I don't know if I ever said thank you in all that drama."

"You did."

"I am a Catholic. I have been for generations, but I find it hard to attend Church. Because all I want to pray for is my gratitude that you killed all those monsters. Somehow, it doesn't seem like something a Christian woman should be praying for."

"I cannot possibly know the extent of your pain or your daughter's pain.

Not a day goes by that I don't wish I could have gotten there even sooner. Of course, if I think about that too much, I start to think about the people who stood in my way, and I want to visit them."

"It means a lot to me that you feel our pain. I am busy trying not to go crazy and to prevent my daughter from suffering any more than she already had, but there is one other victim."

Nicky looked toward the home office of Mr. Allison.

"There was nothing he could have done, but he still feels emasculated. In many ways, even in death, the bad guys won." She confided.

"In a church in front of God, you promised for better or worse. I don't imagine it will get worse than this."

"I guess I had not thought about it that way."

"I am tracking someone who has kidnapped Amanda. The nun that helped us that night. I am going to ask your husband for his help. If he cannot, for whatever legal or ethical reasons, I will accept that. If he cannot, I ask that, you to accept it as well."

There was no further need for words to explain Nicky's request or her acceptance of what he was asking.

WELL, BRADEN, I GUESS this is where you come to collect the pound of flesh owed. Or to teach me the secret mob handshake." Whereas the rest of the Allison house had a light family touch, the office of DA Allison did not. It was cold and business-like and reminded you of an office that should have been in another building at another time. An outdated grey file cabinet sat next to this gray desk. The desk was covered with folders and stacks of papers that clearly reflected a filing system known only to him. The calendars on the wall needed to be updated, surely kept for the sporting events they displayed. The office is a paragon example of an office if you wake up in the mid-nineteen fifties.

"Mr. Allison, I work for Adam and the law offices of Woodbridge, Foster and Klein. They don't collect payment in flesh. And for the record, the client was Costello, not you."

"I apologize if I have offended you. This mess has disrupted so much of our lives."

"I am trying to get married. I talked just a moment ago with your wife on till death do us part." Nicky moved closer into the room and seated himself, not waiting for an invitation.

"She would be the one to talk to, alright."

"I take it she and Amy are seeking treatment for the mental hell they went through."

"Yes."

"What about you?" Nicky's questions sat cold, weighted in the air, waiting to thaw and drop.

"Why should I? They were the ones raped." He said in a shaky voice.

"Despite the actions, you were the intended victim."

"Victim. You mean the taking of my manhood is now on the table for discussion." Nicky seemed to ignore the anger building in the man before him.

"Let me ask you a question. When you drop a heavy weight from a tall building, when does it stop?"

Allison looked confused at the questions and how it had anything to do with the direction of the conversation. "When it hits the bottom, I suppose."

"When I saw what was happening, you and your family, something set itself in motion that could not stop until it found its bottom. Until every one of those animals was dead at my hand. There is a monster that lives in me that can rage out of control. The worst part is that as much as I hate and despise the monster, I love him too because he is the greatest connection to the monster that resides within my sister. So, when I hear you talk, you sound sad to be human it challenges my ability to understand. I have had this monster living in me for as long as I can remember."

By this time, Allison was staring at Nicky. "Being normal and human, you could have done nothing differently. Sometimes, to fight a great monster, you need a greater monster, and the humans must stay the hell out of the way."

"So, Nicky, why did you come today?"

"Because I need your help, and you are free to refuse if it violates some code or law."

"What could you possibly need from me?"

"I need to talk to Papa Lapone. He is being held in protective custody while he rats out the rest of his organization."

"Why?"

"Amanda, the nun that helped me the night you were abducted, is missing, and he doesn't know it, but he can lead me to the people that have her. I must tell you, in all honesty, if whoever has her has hurt her in any way, the information you give me will be used to make sure justice is served. The justice served will not be on paper handed out or in fines. It will be merciless."

"No easy cases for you. I will do what I can, but, in the end, it is his choice, and he may think you are going to take him out."

Nicky stood and reached over the desk and shook Allison's hand, a long, genuine handshake of mutual respect. "One question for you, Braden. Does your fiancée know about the monsters?"

"I think she knows what your wife knows about you, and all wives should know about their husbands. That is, to truly love us, you must learn to love or, at best, tolerate our imperfections."

"Yeah, you are ready for marriage."

Chapter 14

"So, Nicky, before I agree to talk to you about anything, you must tell me why you kicked the crap out of my son Denny." Papa Lapone, a heavy-set, aging, greying gangster being held in an army bunker, asked.

"He was forcing himself on Gail in public."

"So, he married her, didn't he.'

"They weren't married then, and mistreating a woman, even your spouse or potential spouse, is the old way, not the new way." Nicky met the tough-eyed gaze of the seasoned gangster with equal contempt.

"Millennial gangsters, I got to get the book. So, Cole, you are looking good as well. Time for you to pick out a fella and dance down the aisle, isn't it?"

"Working on it." Cole smiled and nodded at Nicky for him to continue his conversation.

"So, Nicky, if that whack job kid of mine didn't talk you into whacking me, what can I do for you?"

"Nothing. But there is something I can do for you."

"You sound confident, young man."

"Someone is committing a crime, and they think they can add it to the things you are being charged with and bury the trail."

"If it's bad, how do you know I didn't authorize it? You know I am the bad guy."

"Because whether you like me or not. Whether I like you are not its immaterial. We are what we are. The people I am tracking are organ harvesting babies from orphanages in poor, war-torn countries and selling the body parts to the highest bidder in the richest nations."

"Mr. Lapone, they are stripping the organs out of live children for profit." Cole further explained with a slight breaking in her voice.

Lapone stared for a moment, not able to form words. "In the name of God, are you tracking down the devil?"

"Probably, and when I find him, his ass or mine. But you have been one thing all your life: you don't want people thinking you had a hand in this when it comes out."

"It's those twins that wanted stuff refrigerated moved everywhere with no concern about the cost. I should have known they were too good to be true."

Chapter 15

"May I help you?" Connie's receptionist asked the Woman entering the office. The Woman is attractive in a mature fashion. Her clothing screamed of the latest designer, and she strolled with an air of aristocracy. She walked an obvious bodyguard. A huge man of mammoth proportions with a beaten and torn look like someone that was not just a bodybuilder but someone that fought to the death on a regular basis and won. He wore a black suit with a turtleneck shirt. His eyes darted about the room in a manner you were not sure if he was surveying possible hazards or having a reaction to bad wiring going on behind his eyes.

"Where do I find Connie Harris?" The Woman tapped on the receptionist's desk as if her full attention was demanded. The receptionist had been in a conversation with Mavis, the Executive Assistant.

"My name is Mavis. I am the executive assistant around here. Is there some way I can help you?"

The Woman stared at the hand offered her, then spoke. "I am sure that's the answer to a question. Just not the one I asked." She broke off eye contact with Mavis and went back to speaking to the receptionist.

"This is a deeply personal matter, and she may not want the help to overhear our conversation."

"Is she expecting you, ma'am?" The receptionist asked, reaching for the phone to contact Connie.

"You really are worthless, aren't you." The Woman walked away toward the offices with Mavis hot on her heels.

"You are actually quite attractive. The picture in the magazine doesn't do you justice." The Woman proclaimed, finding Connie's office, and slamming a business magazine copy with Connie's picture on the front. "I am Vivian. I guess you have heard of me."

Connie looked at Mavis for a clue, but there was none was given.

"You're dismissed," Vivian announced to Mavis. Mavis's eyes popped at the proclamation.

"No. This is my office, and I say who gets dismissed and when. She stays. I may be away for a while, and she has to be up on every aspect of this business." Connie corrected. "Now, if you came to buy into the ongoing projects, you are too late. The truth is we have more investor capital than we need."

"I didn't come here to buy in. I came here because you have something that belongs to me, and I want it back."

The bodyguard still stood surveying the room with a menacing look.

"What is it that you think I have that belongs to you?"

"Nicolas Braden." Vivian quickly answered as if the answer should be obvious.

"Look, Vivian, I got a D minus in gangster arranged marriages and dating protocol, so you may have to bring me along slowly. A little catch-up." Connie's statement had Mavis now staring at Connie as much as the invaders.

"It is simple. I have first refusal, and I don't refuse. I want him. Now, I won't be unfair; I will give you a few million for your inconvenience, and you can find some buff young black strippers to rub oil on you on some sandy beach somewhere to help you heal. But I get Nicky back."

Connie stared at Mavis as if she could translate. "Don't look at me. My mind keeps locking on the buff black stripper thing." Mavis confessed.

"Is this a private party, or can anyone join?" Libby had entered the room unnoticed due to the stun caused by the general direction of the conversation. Libby was wearing one of Cole's former dresses and carrying a purse. Libby had her hand in the purse as if securing something.

"Libby," Connie shouted.

"I brought family," Libby announced, stepping aside, and Holley raced to hug Connie.

"Hey Frankie baby, how's it hanging." Libby addressed the bodyguard.

"You know each other?" Connie asked.

"Yeah. Franklin Stein and I go back away. I remember when he played football."

Franklin made an unhappy growling sound. "Frankenstein," Mavis repeated, trying not to laugh, and failing.

"No Franklin Stein." Libby made a gesture to indicate the breakup of the words.

"Someone actually named this poor guy Frankenstein," Holley asked.

"No, it's more like a stage name. Now, what was the real first name?" Libby pretended not to remember. "Oh yeah, Oliver. Oliver Stein doesn't sound nearly as frightening as Franklin Stein. Can't get villagers all riled up with that name." Franklin turned toward Libby as if he was going to do something to stop her from embarrassing him. Libby removed her hand from her purse and had a .9mm handgun. "This guy I know ended his career goes by the name of Rhino. His real name is Richard Richmond. What do you say, Frankie baby? I set up a rematch."

"I like you better when you dressed like the pizza delivery boy." Vivian snapped, indicating to Franklin it was time for them to leave. "This isn't over. You turn down my offer means I get to go to Dominic." Vivian turned and walked out in grand fashion.

"Who or what is a Dominic, and why do I feel like someone may try to cut off my thumbs," Mavis asked.

Libby took Mavis by the hands. "No, too short we don't need them." And all the women started to laugh.

Chapter 16

M att left the bookstore; he had found the book he had been searching for since the night he and Cole had first made love. A young woman in prison wrote poetry and expressed in her writing how much freedom love gives one's sole. Matt noticed a large man walking behind him and realized he had seen the man before. Matt searched his mind for the man's name, but it illuded him. With his mind filled with the exact way he would introduce poetry to Cole, he lost track of time and space and found himself standing directly in front of his car, searching for his keys. Something hit him, and he was smashed against the car like a freight hitting him from behind. Matt dropped the book. He reached for the book lightheaded and noticed that the big man from before was standing there smiling. Not clear how Matt found himself airborne until he hit the cement parking lot floor with his face. Sideways he flew. Was it a blow or a kick? Did it matter? There was an internal crunch, and he knew something that was never meant to break had broken. But where was the book, he thought. Over there, he saw it. Crawling, he reached it and hugged it, protecting the book from the onslaught his body was taking. Then there was darkness.

"WHERE IS HE?" COLE raced into the emergency room, frantic to find Matt. "I am Annette his sister. The one that called you he keeps asking for you." A young woman of flat body type who looked a lot like

47

Matt rushed to Cole. Nicky was trying to keep pace with his sister, but it was clear she was totally overcome by the news that Matt was in the emergency room calling her name.

"You don't look like any lawyer I ever saw." A woman a little older than Cole remarked, walking up with a woman who looked like the Woman's mother.

"Twins huh. Are your parents in town? My name is Edna I am Matt's mother." The older of the females stated.

"No, mom. Their father died years ago, and their mother disappeared." Annette clarified.

"How do people just disappear?" Tanya, the older daughter, asked.

"It's not our concern," Annette remarked.

Annette pulled Cole to intensive care, where they could view Matt. Matt was a mass of tubes and bandages. His small face peeked out from head bandaging. His defeated eyes looked excited to see Cole, and he motioned for her to approach him. Cole pushed past the doctors and nurses and allowed Matt to whisper in her ear what he had been trying to recall just prior to the beating. "Franklin Stein."

VIVIAN SAT IN THE FRONT of her massive home with guests enjoying a drink and conversation. The evening had just started to fall. A car's engine roared suddenly, and there were the tires squealing. "Everybody inside, now." The lead bodyguard yelled and began grabbing guests and rushing them toward the house. Vivian was in full gallop, running for cover. Franklin stood and gazed at the Mustang convertible that raced through the flower bed. Franklin saw the look on Cole's face as she aimed the car. She was not going for Vivian. She was not going for the important guest. She was after him.

Franklin ran as fast as he could, but his bad the knee did not understand the urgency. Crash. With Libby in the passenger seat, Cole ran into Franklin and bounced off the front of the car. Cole shoved the car into reverse and then gunned the engine as she shifted back into drive. The front of the car did a sideways slide as the rear tires burned rubber. She drove to the left of the running. Franklin slammed on the break and opened the driver's door, spamming him with the door. "Hey, Franky baby, thought I might miss you." Cole and Libby stepped out of the car, popped open steel batons, and walked toward Franklin. He was barely able to stand after being hit twice by the car. He reached for Cole. She ducked beneath his swing, did a spin, and hit him on his bad knee with the baton. There was a combination of crunch and crash as both the giant's knees hit the concrete at the same time. Libby hit his eyes with a wicked backhand swipe, and he let out a howl that was not even close to the normal screams of a human, and the women continued to beat him. At some point, Libby stopped, but Cole seemed incapable of stopping the beating of the now clearly dead giant.

"Stop Cole, he dead already!" Libby screamed at her friend.

"Cole looked at Libby with an anger ragging in her face."

"Stop that shit, Cole. I know what you are feeling more than anyone else."

"Let's just get back to the hospital." Libby's statement had calmed Cole down. "I want to cut her head off." Cole confessed.

Returning to the hospital, Nicky ignored the rumpled look of Cole and Libby as they parked themselves, holding him around the waist from both sides. "I talked to Inez she has a helicopter picking up a surgeon and flying him here on one of the private planes. He will be picked up and helicoptered to the heliport on this building."

"Your kids are so close and so resourceful you must be so proud," Edna said to Holley.

Holley could only smile.

Chapter 17

"**G**ood to see you still want to work as a team player Braden," Winchester announced as the two met in a run-down bar near the FBI office. "Is it as bad as we thought?" Nicky asked. "Worse by far. The CIA says there are several companies that are selling people parts all over the globe. They are big with infinite resources and use mercenaries and gangs to do their wet work."

"Sounds like a country with no walls or borders." Nicky guessed.

"I take it you had no success with Lapone."

"He gave me a direction, but there is something I missed yesterday watching the African Guard."

"What's that?"

"It depends on how fast you can get a search warrant for a stolen car."

THE NIGHT HAD BEGUN to send wind whipping down the building-made cannons of New York to claim its dominance. "So, you guys finally come to see about this abandoned car?" An older black man with thick glasses asked. He was the lot attendant. "Did you see who parked it?" Winchester asked. "Hell yeah. Fine sister with some skinny little white girl. I tried to get the sister's number, but she looked at me like she didn't speak English, imagine that."

Nicky smiled. "Yeah, imagine that." The small group stood with the tow truck operator by a rusted-out Ford parked on the lot that Nicky found the stub for in Amanda's cell. "If you are staying in the hotel, you usually use the underground parking there for free, so why do you need to park here and pay? It's what we were overlooking." Nicky explained.

When they opened the car, they found a remote camera set up to view the hotel entrance. "There is someone they were watching coming and going. We need to process the tape, and then you can run facial recognition. The guys you are looking for may not have records in the US. There should be a set of Dutch or German twins."

"That came from Lapone, I guess."

"They were the ones who didn't seem to mind what he charged to move refrigerated cargo from all over the globe," Nicky explained.

"MR. AND MRS. BROWN, my name is Abigale Thorn. I am the lead medical tech and a surgical nurse here. It is my job to help in various stages of transition."

"What type of transition?" Mr. Brown asked.

"Good question. Recovery in this case. Jonathan is doing very well. He is a fighter, and being well fed and cared for since birth is surely paying dividends in the recovery."

Mrs. Brown looked more excited than she had in months.

"All I would like to do is have you visit him today on a limited basis."

"Why limited?" Mr. Brown asked.

"Because he is recovering, as I said, so he is in a sterilized field. Also, we are building his strength so he may tire even though he may want to visit you until he drops." Abigale smiled.

"Before we go in, really, how is he?" Mr. Brown asked in a cold, sober tone.

"Everything promised is well underway. He is doing great. My only concern at this time is the worried looks on your faces scaring him."

The Browns looked at each other and realized she was right. They had worn the mask of impending death for so long it had frozen on their faces. Now was them to put on the masks of possible life.

LIBBY WALKED TO THE parking lot of the hospital. The surgeon had arrived, and hope was starting to permit Matt's visitors. Still, Cole clung to Holley with feelings of guilt, knowing that the pain Matt felt was her fault.

"Hey, Libby over here."

Libby heard a familiar voice call out to her. It was Josh, one of the bodyguards she knew from California. He was standing next to a limo with the door open. Libby walked over to him. Libby had stepped outside the hospital to breathe and take in all that had transpired since her arrival. "Get in; we need to talk," Josh said, sliding into the limo. Libby sat in the limo facing him. Something was wrong. An alarm went off in her head. Before she could correct the mistake, both limo doors opened, and two very large men got in on both sides of her, sitting unnecessarily close to her.

"Get out and wait by the curb." One of the men commanded Josh. Josh hurried out, careful not to look into the eyes of Libby. In an instant, the limo was off to its destination. "Look, boys, if this is a gang bang, you are in luck; I just happen to bring my glow-in-the-dark extra-large strap-on," Libby remarked, and one of the men grabbed her purse before she could reach into it. "You won't need the gun tonight, honey; this aint that kind of meeting."

The limo stopped in a parking garage across from a different limo and an older man got out. He climbed into the limo facing Libby. There was something familiar about him, but she was not sure what. Libby had always been taught when you are in a dangerous situation, the worst thing you can do is to stop thinking of your outs. But now, her mind was frozen. Who is he, and why does a stranger so compel me? The older gentleman wore fine clothes and had a large gold ring on one of his fingers. Libby looked at the ring, and it was not the ring but his hands that were most prominent. His fingers were long and smooth, like a violinist's or a concert pianist's. She had known only one man with such fine hands. As she looked up, the recognition catapulted forward. This man reflected Franco, the man who had found her in the streets and been partially responsible for her upbringing. Libby could not stop staring at his face, and it took a while to notice he was now handing her brandy he had poured from a decanter that was in the limo's built-in bar. She waited for him to sip his, and then she followed. "Oh god, I have been drinking that rotgut. This stuff is good." Libby commented. A smile came over the man's face, and like a blast of heat, all of Libby's fears evaporated. "How have you been, Libby?" he asked.

"Who are you?"

"I am Alonso. You might say I am your uncle. Franco was my older brother." Libby drank more of the brandy. "If this is some kind of trick."

"No, sweetheart, I am here on a mission from Domonic. Libby had never met Domonic, but she knew who he was. Domonic was the highest ranking of Gangsters who lived in an undisclosed nonextradition country, primarily Domonic was retired but no one challenged his authority or wisdom. Domonic had been helped to flee the country with the Woman he had fallen in love with and two girls they had adopted. He did not want the gangster life for them. Nicky and Nichole had helped Domonic escape arrest and flee the country, and for this, Nick and Nichole were under his protection.

"But I had to see you for myself."

"It almost killed me to watch him die." Libby did not care that with all the hard-boiled toughness she displayed, she was now crying.

"He wrote me letters. Can you imagine what a lost art that is now? But in his letters, he spoke of his love for his found daughter." Alonso took Libby's purse from one of the men sitting beside her and put letters in her purse. "We never know how much someone means to us until it's too late, do we."

"If you knew about me, why didn't you come for me?" Libby thought for a moment about her questions, and minor shame overcame her. What right did she have to be consoled? Few knew the grief she felt at the loss of Franco.

"You had Greta. And I watched you through people."

"You said you are on a mission. Let's hear it." Libby allowed him to refill her glass and fought to regain her composure.

"You and Nicole Braden killed Franklin."

"Fuck him. He needed it."

"Watch your mouth, young lady. And yes, he needed it." Alonso's tone mixed parental scolding and leadership as it rang out.

"I see Nicole going after Vivian and killing her. Vivian is protected the same as Nicole, and this should not happen without permission, which Dominic is not willing to grant."

Even with drinking excellent brandy, the problem was now clearer than ever. "If Cole kills Vivian without permission, someone must kill her. Which will cause a tidal wave of shit, and Nicky will wipe out half the freaking eastern seaboard."

"Again, with the language dear, and yes."

"How do we solve this mess, or does it involve me."

"Yes, in the greatest of ways. First, the computer guy, Matt is a nobody, so Vivian's hurting him should be solved by killing Franklin, another nobody. But if there is one that kills Vivian as the return of a favor granted, Dominic will allow this."

Libby now looked a little lost. "What favor?"

"You know, sweetheart, the thing in Clovis."

"Uncle Alonso, I don't have a clue as to what you are talking about."

"Nicole smoked your brother and his fellow rapist. She burned the bodies. I understand there was evidence of torture. Sounds like her style, don't you think." Alonso smiled, realizing she was not conning him. She had no idea. "I guess she did not think you would ever be free with that demon in your closet."

"Even when she hurts, she treats me like the little sister. She had me sent here out of suspicion if there was an investigation."

"I recommended that you take out Vivian because you and only you would be allowed. That would also make you a protected person after that kill. Under my protection, of course, not Domonic." Libby put down the glass grabbed Alonso's hands, and held her face in them, remembering the memories of his brother. "I accept." She whispered.

"I don't recommend you let Nicole go with you because it could complicate matters." He offered as a final reminder. Alonso got back into his limo, and the limo-carrying Libby returned to pick up Josh. Josh sat across from Libby. It did not take but a second before Libby retrieved the brass knuckles from the purse and began climbing on Josh and punching him in the head.

"I had to," Josh screamed, and he was being beaten. The men stopped the limo. The swerve to the curve knocked Libby off the top of Josh, and she landed on the floor of the limo. One of the bodyguards opened the door and yanked Josh out of the car.

"Look, just because I fucked you a time or two doesn't mean I owe you shit." Libby looked horrified at Josh's comment. Something Holley had said about advertising for the wrong type of people shot through her mind. The large man that had separated Libby and Josh yanked Josh from the limo and stood over him. The bodyguard then pulled his gun and pointed it at Josh's head. The large man then looked at Libby, waiting for her to say yes or no to his pulling the trigger. Libby shook her head no. "Lucky night, punk." He said before kicking Josh a couple of times. "Where to ma'am the large man asked Libby. "Back to the front of the hospital." Libby sat back in the limo and drank another glass of the good brandy she knew she was high, but it was not from the brandy she now knew the high power could bring.

Chapter 18

On the rooftop of a building in downtown New York, Cecil Barr, Donavan Bar, and Abigale sat around a table enjoying a cocktail. The place was a high-priced members-only brothel. The Barr brothers had finished their first round of debauchery. They were waiting for their guest to complete his entertainment and join them. The trio sat in robes supplied by the management. Finally, Colten Walker, or so he now called himself, appeared. He was tall and lean with black, shiny skin and looked like an army ranger, even without a uniform.

"We need to discuss your role in fixing the current problem." Donovan started like it was one of his usual formal meetings.

"No, we don't. We need to start by you, ass wipes acknowledging how badly you screwed up. Thinking you would save a few dollars by not waiting until I freed up has put your nuts in a wringer."

"Look, Mr. Walker, we admit we may have made some errors." Abigale tried to calm the tone of the meeting down.

Chapter 19

"**M**s. Harris, there is a man here to see you. He says it's urgent but doesn't have an appointment." Mavis announced, leading Nicky into the room.

"You cad I should have you thrown out. What did you do to ignite that Vivian woman? No, don't tell me." Connie's voice hid general anger beneath mocking.

Nicky walked up to her and kissed her. Mavis made a move to leave the room. "No, Mavis, I need a witness. Don't leave."

Nicolas got on his bended knee and presented the ring he had been carrying. "Connie Harris, will you marry me?"

"Look, Nicky, if this is to stop me from terminating the pregnancy."

"What," Mavis screamed. Her face was full of shock and horror. She sat down like she had been sucker punched.

"I didn't say I was going to terminate; it is just something I am supposed to think about. Now I feel like the two of you are ganging up on me."

"I got the ring before I knew you were pregnant, so I think it deserves an answer. And by the way, the FBI agent that went with me to pick it out has bigger knuckles than I do, so you must have it sized."

"So why didn't you propose before?" Connie asked.

"Because we are building two houses and starting a business, and I am tracking a couple of mass murderers."

"I somehow think he deserves an answer," Mavis commented. "If it's just to let him up off his knees."

"Yes, Nicky, I will marry you." After they kissed, she asked, "What will you do about Vivian?"

"Very little. Any claim she has goes away when we marry," Nicky answered.

"Did she have Cole's boyfriend beat up?"

"Most likely."

"I don't mean to interrupt, but are you too planning on keeping the baby?" Mavis asked.

"I would love to keep this child if my husband agrees."

"Looks like it's a yes. And thank you, Mavis. I don't think I could have done it without you."

"Doesn't that mean I get to help eliminate ugly names for the child," Mavis asked.

"Nicky, why did you take a man with you to pick our rings?" Connie asked, looking down at the size of the ring.

"It was a woman."

"Damn, she has big hands."

Chapter 20

"**P**lease eat something, Doctor. Then try to see if you can also get your friend to eat. I will bring you some clean water and a towel so the two of you can clean up." Colten announced.

"You killed the Mexicans. I thought you were there to rescue us." The Doctor cried out in a sad tone.

"No, ma'am, they were wild dogs. I am a soldier. The chaos they cause is unnecessary and counterproductive."

"I still won't be able to answer your questions." The Doctor confessed before taking a bite of the food he brought to her new jail cell.

"Right now, I don't need answers. Please feel free to examine her as best you can; she seems so frail." Colten covered Amanda's legs with a blanket as if the sight of her legs was inappropriate for public display.

"You won't hesitate to kill us, will you." The Doctor asked.

"Right now, believe it or not, I hope it does not come down to that. But yes, if necessity calls for it, I will kill the both of you."

"We will die to save the children."

"Then, for your sake, let us pray there is a middle ground to which we can all agree." And he was gone.

LIBBY EXITED THE PLUMBING van and began loading tools onto a dolly. She wore a pair of blue overalls with a name tag that read

Mary. She loaded drywall and paint onto a cart, wrestled with the cart and dolly to the stairs, and then up through the mall lobby. "Excuse me, lady, what is all this? A guard, a large man with a distinctive New York accent, stepped in her way.

"Got to set up for the job so we don't have to shut down the water during business hours," Libby answered.

"Don't tell me you are a plumber."

"No, and I don't want to be one. But my dad and uncle own the company, and I am starting to work in the office. They say, Mary, you can't sit in an office and expect grown men to follow your orders if you've never been in the field."

"Your old man and uncle sound like a couple of smart guys."

"Me, I would like to marry one of these palookas and have a half dozen of his kids."

The Guard smiled. "I think I can see your old man's problem. Why don't you take your stuff up the service elevator? I will unlock it for you."

Chapter 21

Libby put the out-of-order sign on the ladies' room's outer door. Libby had learned by checking with a local bodyguard she had worked with in the past that, every Thursday morning, Vivian came to the Corner Bar early and had a cup of coffee before she went across the street to her broker. Vivian would go to the ladies' room, relieve herself, and check her appearance before strutting across the street. Libby had worked for Savannah, a queen in the mob families, and Libby knew that, unlike Savannah, Vivian employed few female bodyguards. This meant when Vivian went to the lady's room, the male Guard would be posted outside the door instead of someone standing outside the stall. Libby cut drywall to fit the doorway to the storage closet in the ladies' room and a matching cut for the men's room. Libby took down the lady's room mirror that showed the closet entrance, leaving the mirror that showed the stall in its reflection. At the end of the day, Libby entered the closet and fitted the dry-painted drywall into place with her inside. Libby had a snack and played solitaire on her cell phone while she waited for the mall guards to make their final rounds. After the Mall guards made their rounds, she cut the wall into the men's room. She fitted the extra drywall into place, making it look like a wall as well, but before she did that, she took the out-of-order sign from the lady's room and moved it to the men's room. Libby laid back and fell into a light sleep, dreaming about Franco and how he had taught her this type of hit. He called it the Trojan horse. Patience was the best weapon, he would say, much better than spraying the room with bullets and hoping one hits someone. Libby was aware that the remembrances of Franco pushed back the nightmares of her brother, setting her up for rape as a cure for lesbianism.

Like clockwork, one of the first people to enter the lady's room was a set of big burley guards surveying the room before allowing Vivian to enter. "All Clear." One shouted. Libby allowed Vivian time to relieve herself, and when Vivian was washing her hands, Libby stepped out of the created wall space and shot Vivian with a taser. Vivian hit the floor, twitching and unable to speak or call out. Libby then injected her with a tranquilizer. Libby handcuffed Vivian, duct taped her legs together, laid out a tarp, and rolled Vivian into the tarp, tucking the head and feet in place like a giant burrito.

"You are a lot heavier than you look, lady." Libby whispered to the comatose body of Vivian, "Don't worry, I have a plan to help you lose some of that ugly fat." With no great care, Libby loaded the tarp with Vivian onto the drywall cart and rolled it into the men's room through the wall whole. Libby replaced the drywall for the women's room and the men's room. Libby put on a rubber mask of an old man and changed her name tag from Mary to Marty and rolled the drywall out of the men's room door. Libby saw three bodyguards waiting for Vivian outside the ladies' room door. The guards stepped out of her way as she pushed the cart to the service elevator. Libby had made a wax impression key when the Guard had shown her the elevator the day before. The plastic key worked fine. Libby was in the plumbing van with Vivian tucked away in the back in less than ten minutes from when she stepped out of the wall. "Hey. Vivian, I want to thank you for all you are doing for me. Few people would donate their heads." Libby joked, and she hummed the song Sweet Rosie O'Grady expecting no response from Vivian.

"RELEASE ME, YOU TRAMP." These were the first words Vivian could say as he came out of her drug-induced haze. Vivian was bound with her head taped to a plastic milk crate to expose the neck best. "You can't do this. I am protected."

"Well, I can, and as it turns out, I am the only one allowed. I guess this is what power feels like." Libby noted as she sat sharpening a manchette.

"Alright, the jokes are over; let me up."

"No can do."

"Look, if the idea was to scare me, you win. I'm scared. So how much?"

"How much what?'

"How much money do you want to set me free?"

Libby stopped sharpening her manchette and kneeled face to face with Vivian. "I have wiped the butts of people like you for a long time. I walk in your shadow. You call me a freak, but when no one is looking, you slap my ass or cop a feel. Hell, one of you prissy bitches got pissed because I would not stand there and let her shove her hand down my pants. Now I get to be in the position of power, and there is no way you will take that away."

Vivian started to cry. "If you are doing this for Cole, she wouldn't kill for you."

"Crying won't help. I freed your mouth in case you wanted to pray; don't waste the time you have left. And by the way, she already has."

Libby stood behind Vivian, and Libby's shadow fell over Vivian. Vivian began to pray, and with one downward thrust, Vivian lost her head. Libby scooped it up, put it in a plastic bag, threw it in the van, and was on her way while the body was still twitching.

Chapter 22

"She prays a lot. She has been praying all morning." Colton observed talking to Doctor Ottumwa.

"She is a nun, and they pray a lot." The Doctor sapped.

"They raped a nun. Those animals. I hate this job more and more."

"It has historically happened before."

"Tell her I won't rape her no matter what happens going forward."

"She is not praying for herself. She is praying for your soul. She says the dead men are lucky. Braden now comes for you."

"HEY BRADEN, WE GOT a hit on the twins on Amanda's video. They are Cecil and Donovan Bar, and right now, they are in town. We have to be careful because they are the kind of guys who can go on international flight faster than most people could catch a bus." Winchester beamed into Nicky's phone. "Israel is really pissed with this pair, and we can get some international goodwill just dragging their asses in."

"We can always hope they resist."

"I will pick you up in half an hour. Try to remember your gun."

"WHERE IS THE CAMERA that goes with the remote?" Colton asked.

"In the belly button of the little teddy bear that sits in the back window of that raggedy blue Ford, we parked across from the hotel entrance," Amanda answered in a labored voice; she was now physically doing better. She knew there was no longer a need to withhold the information. Braden would have found it by now, and he would be coming soon.

"The police may have that car by now," Coltan exclaimed.

"Which means they will go for your bosses, and your boss will point the finger at you. Isn't that how this all works? You are a soldier. You raid the wrong village. No one above you take the hit. It is all left on you." The doctors' words were sharp and cut into the experiences of Colton.

"But Nicky isn't a cop. He is a killer. He is going to hurt you." Amanda said in a matter-of-fact voice. "

"You should consider making a deal." The Doctor offered.

"What."

"You didn't create this mess, and when they couldn't find you, they found wild dogs to replace you. What does that say about how they feel about you?" The Doctor remarked. There was an uncomfortable shifting of who was in control.

"I HEAR YOU KILL PEOPLE, so I guess we have much in common." The unrecognized voice spoke to Nicky on his cell phone.

"How can I help you," Nicky asked.

"I have something you want, and I want to know if it is worth my while to give it back to you."

"You have Amanda and the doctor, and you want to know if I can fight the urge to kill you if you give them back."

"She cries out for you. Are you her best friend?"

"What are you asking?'

"Look, those freaky twins have billions; guys like us just do their dirty work. You and I could go to jail for the rest of our lives any day. Those creeps and that Abigail chick live in luxury. All I want is for you to back off long enough for me to scare them out of some of that cash. I can even give you a cut. Send it by your girlfriend."

"I am going to hang up now," Nicky responded.

"Look, don't be such a fucking hard ass. Those twins screwed this up. I am trying to fix it." Nicky disconnected the line.

"HE IS GOING TO MAKE it, but the road back to anything that resembles normal is long and hard." Dr. Chan, Matt's primary Doctor, explained this to Nicole and Matt's sisters. "You must be a very special girl to have so many people rushing to get everything taken care of for Matt." His mother noted. The group stood around Matt's bed, him having been moved to a private room. "I am sorry I referred to the kid as your children a time or two; it's just that you seem like so much more than an aunt to Nicky, Nichole, and Libby." Matt's mother observed, and the pride overload prevented Holley from responding. Holley's cell phone went off. "It's your brother who needs you to watch his back. Go, we got things covered here." Holley informed Cole.

Chapter 23

S top wiggling, Bitch." Libby uttered as he punched Abigail in the face with brass knuckles. Cole and Libby sat in the back of the plumbing van with Abigale bound on the floor between them. Nicky had informed Cole of the information he needed from Abigail to give him the tactical advantage over the people holding Sister Amanda and Doctor Ottumwa. Libby and Cole also collected the information that would assist Agent Winchester in her upcoming raid of the transplant offices.

"Where have you been all night, young lady?" Cole asked Libby in a stern voice.

"I had something to do."

"Well, at least I hope you used a condom. Maybe two; this is New York."

The big sister tone of Cole made Libby smile.

"I met a guy." Libby started.

"Meeting is nice." Cole kicked Abigail partially out of frustration and partially because she saw it as fun.

"The guy is Alonso. He is Franco's younger brother. He was sent here to give me a go-ahead to deal with Vivian."

Cole stared in shock at Libby. "And you didn't think you should take me for backup?"

"No. He said if you were involved, it could start a war. I had permission because I was repaying you for what you did in Clovis."

Cole attempted a disguised innocence but quickly abandoned it. Cole pulled out her switchblade knife and looked into the eyes of Abigail.

"Have you ever wondered what those children feel when you cut stuff out of them? Well, wonder no more."

Abigail began bucking. Her mouth was bound, but you could hear her trying to plea. Abigails, please, were the useless plea of the damned.

"I am sorry I had not told you yet, but it was for the best," Cole told Libby.

"I know. And Vivian lost her head in our last meeting."

Cole began stabbing Abigale, and blood spurted.

"He is setting me up with an allowance, and I don't have to go back to California unless you think I should." Libby tested the waters.

"No, you are going to stay here with us. Holley must teach us how to be Aunts."

Cole and Libby set the van on fire with the dead body of Abigale in it as waves of smoke and evidence lofted through the air. Cole and Libby walked away with Libby humming 'When Irish Eyes Are Smiling.' "I guess we are stuck with each other as friends now, let's go help Nicky," Cole observed. Cole swiped her hair, flipping it from her face, and Libby recreated the same hair flip. "Kid, maybe there is hope for you yet."

Chapter 24

Cecil walked down the hallway toward his office. He had gotten a tip that the FBI might be interested in some of his transactions, and he was busy having his people code information so that it would not show up in a normal raid. Rushing down the hall, a hand grabbed and shoved him into the stairway. "Hi, we haven't met. My name is Nicolas Braden, but everyone calls me Nicky." Nicky shot a right punch to Cecil's face that snapped his head back. Cecil tried to step away from the wall, and Nicky hit him with a left, followed by a head butt. Cecil's mouth and nose started bleeding. "Take off your tie." Nicky screamed at Cecil.

"What?'

"Nicky punched him again. My shrink says I should be less hostile, but you, being a mass murderer and all, I am fairly sure she will write me a day pass." Nicky drew back to hit him again, and Cecil removed his tie.

"You will tell me where Sister Amanda and the Doctor are. You will tell me every little coding trick I need to know to locate the places where the children and the money are hidden."

"You don't understand this is a big business."

"You don't understand your life means a lot less to me than those children. Right now, I might find beating you to death quite relaxing."

69

FOR THE FIRST TIME since Colten had been taking off the book missions, he felt he was involved in one he might be unable to salvage. He had brought in two pros to help him, Rex and Lasso, but they might not help. The problem wasn't simply that the Mexican Gangbangers had silenced the one person that could tell where the physical camera that went with the remote control that had been found with Amanda and Doctor Ottumwa, but that they were running out of time and Cecil and Donovan had no appreciation for the hard work of others.

"Why don't we just pull up stakes? You don't owe those two clowns anything." Rex asked. Rex was a mercenary that looked more like a high school science teacher. He was tightly compacted in build and barely six feet, but he knew systems and software. Rex was not happy with the mess that had been created. Lasso, a tall, muscular man, paced. Lasso had military hair and a stern look about himself. "We work the mission. We get out alive; that's the way it always works."

"Bring me my money. I got the little one to talk. But you are not going to like what she had to say." Colten told Donovan on the phone.

"I KNOW YOU." DR. OTTUMWA called out as Donovan entered the room. "You are the benefactor that sought only to help the children live better lives."

"Don't mock me. Does the lion apologize to the gazelle on your Kalahari Dessert? No, he realized survival favors the strong. You are weak and must fuel the strength that we evolve to a greater world. It is best for everyone."

"For generations, Colonizers have justified their evil actions just as you have," Amanda said in little more than a whisper. Still, it rang a chill in the air around Colten.

"Do you agree with him, Colten. Was your grandmother and her mother raped for the greater good of colonizers." Amanda asked more clearly. Donovan walked over to Amanda and drew back his hand to slap her, and Colten grabbed his hand in midflight. "You are losing; she is winning," Lasso stated to Donovan. "She sacrificed herself to give time for the information to be retrieved to be worthless, and now they are both lying there pressing your every button." Lasso walked over to Colton. "We have our money. He has his answer. It's his mess from here."

REX WALKED THE PERIMETER, relieved that this assignment was almost over. Fixing a botched job was the worst. No one gave you credit for the good you did. They only complained about the bad job the people before you did. Rex saw two young ladies in similar business suites walking toward him. They were attractive, and he thought they might want to party with the money he would be earning from this short job.

"Excuse me, I think my little sister got us lost." Cole started.

"You can't tell a strange guy we are lost. He might want to take advantage of us." Libby took her cue.

"What are you young ladies looking for?' Rex asked. Libby pulled out a piece of paper to show Rex. Rex leaned forward to read the paper, and Cole stabbed him in the throat with her switchblade. Cole and Libby gently rested him on the ground as Nick walked up.

"How far out is Winchester?" Cole asked.

"We got seven to ten minutes. Let's make it work."

"Roger that," Libby responded.

THERE WAS AN EXPLOSION that rang and echoed. The sound of metal flying through the room followed the explosion. The smell of burning cordite filled the air, and the electric system flashed. "That must be the FBI. I don't know how they found this place." Donovan said in a sad, quivering voice.

"That aint the FBI; it's her boyfriend," Colten said, staring at the now glowing eyes of Amanda.

"Can you calm him down? Maybe we can cut a deal. He likes money, doesn't he?" Donovan began to bargain.

"He's not here for money, and there aint no way to calm a man down after what happened to her," Lasso stated, walking toward the front of the building. Lasso was confrontable with the dark. He had seen a dozen dark jungles and swamps. His eyes operated just as well in the darkest of places as it did in bright sunlight. He saw a figure standing in front of him. "They say you kill. I say you should let us walk. The guys that hurt your woman are dead." Lasso raised the barrel of his automatic weapon toward the figure and heard a click to his right. His eyes rotated to the right, and there was a light flash. I was the last thing he would ever see.

"Get out there and stop him; that's what we pay you for," Donovan screamed at Colten.

"Hey, Braden, what do you say? You and me. One bad guy against another. No fucking good guy to fuck things up." Colten laid down his automatic rifle and pulled out his combat knife. He walked into the dark, his eyes met Nicky's, and they began to fight in the dark. Colten dropped the knife during the battle, and he could see it shining in a sliver of light. He saw Nicky near him, but the knife was closer. Colten went for the knife, and as he turned around to stab Nicky, Nicky stabbed Colten with Coles switchblade. The men continued to fight without regard for personal injury.

The fight between Nicky and Colton was long and hard, and finally, Nicky was planted on Colton's chest, beating him in the face. Colten looked more dead than alive, and Nicky looked less human than a man should. Cole came to Nicky and rubbed her hand across his shoulder.

"Nicky, stop. Please don't kill him. I got her." And then Cole rested his head on Nicky's back, and he seemed to return to a more human state.

"What the fuck was that. One of you turns into the wolfman, and the other has to stop it." Exclaimed Winchester, walking up and observing the connection between Cole and Nicky.

"Winchester, you got the raid. You got the hostages, and you even got this piece of shit. So let it rest. And by the way, when is the FBI opening its first charm school? Cause gee, they really need one." Nicky grunted.

There was a shot from the automatic rifle that Colten had left in the room where Amanda and Ottumwa were being held. Cole rushed to the room. Cole led Amanda and the doctor out of the room. There was no need to lead Donovan out; he was now dead.

"The thing I want most in this world is to hug you," Amanda said to Nicky as Libby helped him from the floor.

"You must honor our deal." Nicky reminded her with a reassuring smirk.

Amanda burst into tears as Cole led her and Dr Ottumwa out of the warehouse.

"What is your deal?" Libby asked Nicky when no one else could hear.

"We remain friends as long as there is no physical contact."

SO, BRADEN, A FUNNY thing happened during the raid today."

Winchester was leaning against the ambulance where they were tending to a minor injury Nicky had incurred.

"Do tell."

"Well, one of the warrant squads entered the stairwell and found Cecil. It seems he was so overwrought with guilt or afraid of what we would find in his records that he hung himself."

"Well, all's well that ends well." Nicky joked.

"Of course, he beat himself up pretty bad before doing it. You wouldn't want to shine a little light on that, would you."

Nicky looked around like he was considering it. "Nope."

"Which one of your crew shot Donovan?" She asked.

"Don't know off hand I was wrestling with some guy with a knife at the time."

"Another suicide?'

"Winchester, once you start going over those transactions and pulling people in for charges, no one is going to care how those twins ended their lives, just that the courts won't be spending millions trying to try them."

"So does this mean we are friends, and I get an invitation to the wedding.'

"Only if the FBI opens a charm school and you are the first graduate."

Chapter 26

Libby drove up to the undisclosed meeting site. One the bodyguards got out and opened the trunk. Libby threw a plastic bag containing the head into the trunk with no ceremony. She then went and rested, leaning against the limo, and Alonso got out holding two glasses of the brandy he knew she liked and handed her one. "So, it is done."

Libby smiled and nodded. "Did you want to come and live with me? Would you like a home of your own? Just tell me what pleases you." Libby could feel a rush of warmth and trust. She suddenly became aware that the warmth and trust were rushing both ways, that Alonso had a loneliness that called out for family. Now it was clear that it was not only Libby afraid to cry, but Alonso also had tears he was trying to hold back. "Every time I look at you, I want to cry. I miss him so much. The letters were such a reminder of how we struggled to find a loving balance. He wanted a son, and I tried to be that at one point until he let me know it was not necessary to be anything other than what I wanted to be." Libby put her arm around Alonso's waist.

"Everything he has or was willed to him is yours. I have made a large deposit in a bank in your name, and you will receive a regular allowance. Welcome home." Alonso gave Libby a card with the banking information she would need.

"For now, I think I need to stay with Cole. She teaches me so much. Besides, there is a wedding to prepare for, and I want to dress in a knockout dress made by my Aunt Holley." Alonso smiled. "Well, in that case, do you think you might need a date for the wedding."

"I would love that."

Alonso and Libby talked for a while longer about their lives. Alonso told Libby stories of when he and Franco were boys that captivated her in a way she had not felt before. Alonso has two sons. One who wants nothing to do with him as he is a concert pianist. The other son is in prison for murder; he killed a man in a bar in front of fifty witnesses, and no one could intervene and stop him from serving time.

"I need you to at least visit the house regularly to get a feel for the setup. The Grim Reaper will track me down someday, and I am adding you to my will."

"That's not necessary." Libby protested.

"Yes, it is all I owe to my brother Franco. You are, by default, his only child. Besides, you may be called upon to sit as a referee between my sons. You cut off heads. So that should be a walk in the park."

"You and Aunt Holley are changing my life so much it's a lot to take in."

"I only want you to be sure you consider the options open today. They will provide for you in the future. And to fully answer your earlier question on why I did not come to you when my brother first died. I was fearing you would reject me for having been the one to take care of him as he deteriorated. We had suffered a riff in our relationship caused by circumstances that no longer matter."

"It wasn't a misery I could define or share, but it burned a place in my heart." Libby smiled, a little surprised at how, after reading the letters from Franco, she was able to express better how she felt. "A while back, I lost a friend, and another friend of mine said the best way to deal with unresolved issues regarding someone who has passed is to sit down and write them a letter. I think I am going home and writing Franco a letter telling him how much he still means to me."

"NICKY, THAT'S RIDICULOUS it can't be done," Connie yelled at Nicky when he told her the wedding might have as many as 300 people. "Actually, for all families not to be offended and the law enforcement and political people that will be expecting to be invited, I am thinking close to 500." Adam corrected.

Chapter 27

"Please come this way. Adam will be with you in just a moment. He has the FBI and the Representatives from the Church on the phone all day." Inez led Nicky, Cole, and Libby into the Adams office. Adams's office was plush. The room was huge with overstuffed calves, skin leather furniture, and a complete bar. Adam had a mammoth desk with four guest chairs. In one corner, there was a conference table that seated 12.

"We haven't met, but I am Inez." Inez eye Libby. Libby had chosen to dress in a women's business suit that matched what Nicky and Cole were wearing. Libby extended her hand.

"I'm Libby." Inez pushed Libby's hand aside and embraced her with a full hug.

"Look here, you don't greet me that way." Libby smiled and took in the older woman's hug. It was an overwhelming feeling of acceptance.

"Well, you guys are getting to be the talk of the town." Adam led, and Libby, Nicky, and Cole sat on the sofa facing him. Libby had taken her chosen place on the left of Nicky while Cole sat at his right. Libby had no problem not sitting in this place whenever Connie was available. "Business first. Alonso has informed me that he would like to assure you that your connection to his family is permanent and clearly legally defined. I have provided some services for him in the past, but you are clear to choose any legal representation you choose." Adam smiled at Libby. Libby blushed slightly, fighting the notion of daydreaming of the closeness she and Franco had shared. "You will be just fine, Sir." Nicky put his arm around Libby to support her in making her own decisions.

"Now, two. The FBI is shutting down a wellspring of operations connected to the Barr brothers. They are freezing assets and are awash in a tidal wave of legal mess. They are appointing an agent, Winchester, to spearhead the operation. Much of what they have to deal with is that this probe may have been, at best, slowed down here, but it is still international and beyond what we can do."

"For now, we take the small victories," Nicky stated.

"And now for matters of the heart. How is Matt?" Adam asked. Nicole rested her head against her brother and thought for a moment.

"He is better, but there is much to be done. He needs rehab and support. I am going to be there for him every step of the way. I want his sisters to understand." There may have been more that Cole would say, but she chose not to.

"And you. I hear there is a baby and wedding in store. I guess that means I get to buy a new suit." Adam smiled.

"I'll say, you see, Connie has never been close to her family. She got married at an early age to get away from home. She is wondering if you would give her away since you are responsible for the direction, we are going in." Adam rested back in his chair, waiting for the questions he knew Nicky would ask.

Finally, Nicky asked it. "What about Sister Amanda?" Libby and Cole clutched Nicky, showing their support to the next item on the agenda. "Nicolas, there is a facility where traumatized nuns can go. They receive treatment and support. The place is not commonly known and not discussed. You may never see her again. I want you to know I take full responsibility for cutting your correspondence with her. I should have known you could make gentlemanly decisions without my input."

Chapter 28

"Do you know who I am?" Alonso asked Holley. She had been escorted to the dinner surreptitious dinner they had planned. She was dressed in a plain black dress. It had been so long since she had been on a date if this is what this was. Holley found Alonso handsome and well-kept for a man of his age.

"You are Alonso Pettibone." She answered as simply as possible. Alonso insisted she be picked up and driven by limo to the restaurant. The wait staff seemed totally at his command inside the dark, elaborately decorated restaurant. Words seemed almost unnecessary when he had a wish or desire for them to satisfy.

"True, Mrs. Anderson, that is my name, but do you know who and what I am?"

Alonso brushed back his salt pepper greying hair and stared directly at Holley. Holley fidgeted with the real answer for only a moment.

"You are a Gangster and murderer."

Holley's candor caused Alonso to smile. He relaxed in his chair and made a motion, and a waiter appeared and took their orders. "Thank you for that clear assessment. I always feel a little better when two people discussing common interest have the same facts in front of them. So yes, I am a Gangster and Murderer. And so much more."

"So why secretly have me brought here? I have nothing you want or need. I am a simple woman enjoying her later years."

Alonso looked around the room at the other guests while organizing his thoughts. "I have two messages. One is from Dominic, and the other is from me." Even though Dominic lived in a non-extradition country, he was known to run the main crime families in the U.S. Holley had never met him but knew of the great span of his influence.

"Well, Mr. Pettibone, may I say you are the best dress messenger I have ever seen." Holley attempted to ease the moment.

She sipped a glass of wine from in front of her.

"Thank you. And please call me Alonso. I assure you we are not at odds."

"Then please call me Holley. It has been so long since anyone has asked me out personally. Without Nicky and Cole, I was intrigued." Holley now clearly relaxed a little. Holley knew being a simple Midwestern person, she needed to be clearer on etiquette for dining with underworld dignitaries.

"Dominic would like to pick up the tab for the upcoming wedding of Connie and Nicky. It will be one of his gifts to them."

"May I ask why? That is if you are allowed to tell me."

"I was sure you would ask that is why I chose such a relaxed setting. However, as a long-time widow and I being a long-time widower, we fumble at what should be polite conversation. When we get to the tough stuff, I will muck it up."

Holley smiled and gave a slight laugh. He was feeling the same embarrassment that she was feeling. But how could such a man?

"Do you know who Savannah Janus is?"

"I have heard of her." Holley had heard quite a bit about Savannah Janus but was not sure it was a good idea to show how much you knew about the inner workings of organized crime to anyone, especially an admitted murderer.

"The Janus family were old school organized crime. Savannah and her generation are pulling the organized crime world out of the dark shadows and making legitimate businesses that serve the country and investors. Connie is a part of that chain." Alonso paused surely to survey her face to see how much of this was news to her.

It took a moment and the rest of the wine in the glass for Holley to realize the repercussions of what was being said.

"Wait a minute, are you saying that the child Connie is carrying is seen in the Mob world as some sort of messiah to help lead all you lowly gangsters to a promised land through genetic evolution."

Alonso clearly tried his best not to laugh at her making fun of him, but he could not. "Sounds stupid when you say it like that. But the fate of both of Nicky's children is important."

Holley reached for her wine glass and noticed it had not yet been refilled, then took Alonso's from his hand and drank the contents.

"Slow down. What, both children?" Holley's voice was still dry when it finally formed the question.

"I am sorry if I have in any way let the cat out of the bag. I only assumed Nicky would have confided in you. After dinner, we will go over it more slowly."

Holley ate fast, always keeping her eye on Alonso.

Alonso seems to enjoy her attention as well as having the upper hand in a conversation.

"Savannah Janus is pregnant and has not announced the father, but smart money says it was Nicky on that last California job he did."

"But it's a rumor, and you don't know it to be true?"

Holley thrashed about for understanding.

"No, only they would know. But judging from your reaction, if the child is Nicky's, he may not know she is carrying it."

"What's a secret meeting without a lot of secrets?"

Again, Holley's Midwestern candor shot through Alonso's defense, and he chuckled.

They ate dessert and relaxed in each other's company more than in the initial meeting.

"So, what is the request that is personal?" Holley finally asked.

"Please let me explain by telling you a story." Alonso began. "As you know, Libby has been visiting me occasionally. I have been teaching her the legitimate side of the business and how the household is run. The other day I was picking her up for a meeting with an important businessman, and she came into the dressed in her I am bi-sexual, take me or leave me outfit."

"Oh my," Holley exclaimed with a look of pity on her face.

"She froze, then excused herself and returned wearing a beautiful dress you made for her, if I am not mistaken." Alonso stopped and swallowed as if he had made his primary point.

"So, what's the problem."

Alonso leaned forward and took Holley's hands. "My dear, I did not ask her to change. She read it to me. Moreover, she read that I did not want to argue my point. She complied."

"You mean like a loving niece."

Holley's comment showed the terror that Alonso felt.

"So, mister, I am the bad guy. How do you deal with the fact that inside herself, she is rapidly starting to see you as a family? And she doesn't mind that your flaws overshadow hers."

Alonso sat and stared at an aquarium in the room for a moment, then responded without looking at Holley. "Do you know how Libby comes to be seen as my nice? My brother found her when she was a child eating out garbage cans. Her brother had set her up to be raped and sodomized, then disposed of her." When Alonso looked back at Holley, he saw the tears in her eyes through the tears in his own. "My request Aunt Holley is to please help me not fuck this up. I made such a mess with my own two boys. If I got a shot at someone loving me the way she is starting to." He paused. "How many new starts do people our age get?"

"I went through this with Nicky and Cole. I guess they teach us to be caring, loving parents. Whether we deserve it or not. I promise to help all I can, but keep in mind that Cole is her role model, so she will never be the Virgin Mary."

This time, the laugh of Alonso was different. It was not a nervous laugh but one of relief.

"I will ask of you the same as I ask from Nicky and Cole. Be fair to her and honest with me when you can. I don't expect you to give me details that compromise anyone." She added. A simple handshake did not seem quite enough to suffice, but for two out of practice at dating, the meeting overtones had to serve. Had she joined a conspiracy?

And how to approach Nicky about possibly a second child carrying his DNA.

Chapter 29

The return to Sexton, Missouri, and the new Braden home showed great promise. Everyone involved had their pet projects. Connie was busy setting up a nursery for the coming child. Cole was setting up a bedroom for herself when she was staying over and helping Libby set up a room for herself. Nicky spent much of his time in the office that was being set up for himself and the one being set up for Connie. Mavis had come to help set up and to find out what she would need to know from Connie when she would not be available—a beehive of activity.

"NICKY, HOW'S IT GOING these days?" The caller's voice on the cell phone took a moment for him to recognize.

It was Betina, the head of security for Savanah Janus in California. Savannah Janus if the head of an organized family. Savannah is known to be hard to get along with. Nicky had done work for them in the past at the behest of the Law firm he works for.

Nicky and Mavis had been attempting to set up an internet copier and printer in the joint area between his home office and Connie's.

"As well as expected,"

"I am a little busy, so I will jump right in. I have a question to ask you, and if you don't want to answer, it will be fine.

"Shoot," Nicky stated, noticing Mavis's eyes open wide. Mavis is Connie's executive assistant and good friend.

Mavis has always been a little leery about what Nicky and his twin sister do. "Not that type of shoot." Nicky covered the phone and whispered to Mavis to ease her mind.

"Are you about going to be a father sometime soon?"

Nicky wasn't sure how Betina had heard. "Yes."

"I thought you had better taste than that. How could you screw that bitch?"

"Slow down Betina. What did Connie ever do to you?" Nicky was shocked and horrified at her comment.

Betina started laughing uncontrollably. "Congratulations, but I was asking about your popping off a shot of juice into Savannah."

"What the hell are you smoking?"

"Look, buddy, Savannah is pregnant, and the Vegas odds say you are the daddy. The next guy down on the list of prospective donors would be my late husband, and I thought this call would, no matter how disgusting, ease my mind."

Nicky sat looking at the pull-out diagram for the internet copier, and Mavis came over and turned it right side up for him. "The dirty little butt wipe."

"Which one?" Betina asked.

"My twin sister. She knows which way is up. Let me call you back."

"Don't take too long; there is a big betting pool, and I could use a new car."

Nicky disconnected the phone and stared at Mavis for a moment. "Don't you hate it when your Dizygotic twin holds out on you?"

"Can I assume that to be a rhetorical question, sir?"

Chapter 30

"The tailor will need to measure all the men from the wedding party. The best man I understand is in a wheelchair, and Cole's boyfriend uses a cane or walker?" Alonso sat across from Holley at the Hilton, where he was staying. She had been uncomfortable about meeting him at his hotel and had waited for him in the lobby, refusing to go to his suite.

"This all sounds so expensive."

"Don't worry about money. You should never worry about money again." Alonso smiled a little and found his gaze lost in Holley's face, only to turn away when she noticed him looking at her. "How is my niece?"

Holley now gave a full smile at Alonso's question. "She is great and just the thing to keep Cole's head on straight. Libby is visiting you later today, so I think it best that I am not here."

"Why?" Alonso had sat scribbling on a notepad. He now stopped and stared at her.

"I wouldn't want her to think we were secretly dating."

"Am I so repulsive?" Alonso asked clearly offended.

Holley clearly knew she had insulted him. "No. As a matter of fact, you are handsome, charming, and smart. It's just that." And she stopped short of a full explanation.

"It is just that you find me hideous as a general rule."

Holley smiled. "No, Alonso, I have only been with one man in my life, and I get the feeling that even if I were to try to be more than a friend, you would be greatly disappointed."

"Then, my dear Holley, I have a solution. We share children as an interest. And the future. So why don't we try first being friends and not being so quick to judge each other? We have much to cover before I return to the shadows, where monsters such as I dwell."

Now Holley found herself fully laughing. There was something special in this Alonso, or at least in him now that Libby controlled his heartstrings.

"ARE YOU SURE YOU DON'T mind if I go to Clearwater with Cole?" Libby asked Alonso as they sat at dinner in the restaurant inside his hotel.

"I would prefer you stay, but I am reasonable, and I will save my contesting and pouting for a later point. Besides, you can learn much at the hands of the Braden's."

"We are just going to babysit some spoiled rich kid turned actor. Just long enough for the picture he is making to be completed, and the people that fronted the money get their return on their investment."

"I see now, my dear, you talk of return on investment. You are already learning." Alonso smiled the simile of a man noting his achievement.

"Uncle Alonso, can I ask you a favor?" Libby looked ashamed to be asking a favor, considering the short time of their relationship.

"Anything."

"Go and see Aunt Holley. She sometimes seems so lonely, and after the two of you meet for wedding planning, she seems so much happier." Libby reached over and took Alonso's hand and rested it against her face. He even smelled like Franco; the man most responsible for raising her. Libby knew how abrasive she could be, but Alonso did not seem to mind.

"You are not trying to play matchmaker, are you," Alonso said in jest.

"No. But she is nice and at times you both seem lonely."

Chapter 31

Cole and Libby stood at the buffet table in the lounge area set up for the people working in the film. It had been a long flight with no real food, and both women were hungry. Cole reached for a canopy, and a hand grabbed her by the butt before she could reach the food. Cole turned around and noticed Bradly Winters, the pictures star, smiling at his achievement. Cole casually picked up a spoon, then walked over to the hot food on the buffet and picked up a can of canned heat. She popped the top with the spoon and walked back to Bradley, smiling. She put the canned heat in his jacket pocket and then set it on fire by throwing a lit can of the product at him. He went up in flames. She then began flipping scoops of the contents of canned heat containers. Bradley had no choice but to strip and douse himself with a picture of cold water that was on the tables. A bodyguard ran into the room and reached for Cole, but the bodyguard dropped on the floor, twitching from Libby's stun gun. The crowd of workers cheered as Bradley ran naked, screaming from the room.

"I WANT THE FREAKING bitch arrested." Cole walked over to where Bradley was sitting and punched him in the face, causing his nose to spurt blood. Bradley's bodyguard made a move like he was going to stand up and defend Bradley, then noticed Libby eyeing him with a ruthless smile and sat back down. Cole and Libby sat in the office of the film's producer, Morton Spooner, with Bradley, his bodyguard, and Bradley's agent and manager, Leslie Spooner. Bradley was wrapped in a blanket, shaking.

"Look, Brad, dear, remember when I told you this movie was running way over budget, and you told me to relax. Then I need you to relax now and let me explain the facts of life."

Leslie smiled and looked at her charge while Cole and Libby sat and devoured the food they had taken from the buffet. "You see, kid, you needed nine million to finish the picture, and no bank would lend it to you. No collateral, and the loan term was too short for those pirates to make it worth their while."

"So, you went to gangsters?" Bradley shouted in total disbelief.

"Gangsters have backed U.S. films since the twenties; don't sound so puritanical." Leslie enlightened.

"And they sent these charming little dolls as enforcers."

"No. You complete idiot, we weren't sent by the gangsters. We were sent by the lawyers involved. So, they get paid. If you fuck up, the guys that come after we leave won't just set your ass on fire." Cole corrected.

"Over nine million dollars, you would be surprised how enthusiastic the varsity team can get," Libby stated with her mouth full.

"Oh God, can somebody save me," Bradley called out.

"That is why I am here. First, you are high as a Georgia Pine. You celebrate the victory, not the road to the victory. No more drugs until you finish the shoot. No sex. No booze." Cole started.

Leslie could see the fear in Bradley's eyes. His shaking visibly increased. A cold sweat formed on his forehead.

"Look, honey, he has an addiction problem. He can't do cold turkey. I will personally put him in treatment after the shoot, but if you shut him down, he won't stop throwing up long enough for a shoot. And if he hangs himself, no one gets paid. "Leslie bargained.

"Alright, never let it be said I am unwilling to negotiate. One drug if the day shoot is successful. One hooker every two days if he can string two good days together." Cole compromised.

"We search your trailer and your house and remove any temptation. We strip search the hooker, and if she is got anything shoved up in her other than a napkin or a toy, we set ass her on fire."

Libby added, and Cole smiled in approval.

"Look, Brad, you got two, maybe three weeks tops; how bad can that be? Besides, look how real the dramatic seems of your suffering are going to be." The producer smiled, chewing on an unlit cigar.

For Bradley, the next week was pure hell, and the second week was more of the same. But his work was better than it had ever been. The work of his costars also improved, knowing there was an off switch to Bradley's unprofessional behavior in the form of Cole and Libby.

"SAVANNAH, IT HAS TAKEN over a week to get you on the phone. I was considering flying out there to speak with you personally, but who knows what rumors that might cause." Nicky sat in the new home office; glad he had had the room soundproofed.

"Nicky baby isn't that what my other favorite physio calls you."

"Savannah, let's talk rumors."

"Oh. Well, I was going to call you about that. I need a little favor."

"Savannah, Connie is pregnant for the first time and has mood swings. This is not something I want her to hear on a downswing."

"I can relate to the mood swing thing. Now, here is the favor. When someone asks you if you hit the ball over the plate, in my case, I want you to do that old I cannot confirm or deny bit."

"Why, who's kid is it?"

"Gee, you and your sweet sister have been hanging out with lawyers too long. She set the whole thing up, bless her violent little heart."

"Savannah, it is client business; she isn't supposed to tell me you are."

"Oh, very well, if you promise to keep it a secret until I make the announcement. It is Jackie's."

"Your cousin?" Nicky exclaimed in disbelief.

"Technically, I think he is my half-brother. But how's that for a hoot? Any idea on baby names?"

CONNIE HAD NOTICED Nicky moping around the house most of the day. Something was on his mind, but she had no way of guessing.

"Come to the garage with me." Nicky finally requested.

There was a beige compact car in the garage that Connie had never seen before. Nicky handed her the key.

"Gee, is this what you have been frying your brain over all day? You bought me an ugly little car." She laughed. "I appreciate it, not that I need another car."

"I didn't buy the car, it's a wedding present for you."

"From whom?"

"It doesn't matter."

"So, I still want to know." She insisted.

"A group of people you wouldn't know."

"So why would they send me a present?"

"Open the trunk."

"Why." Now Nicky just smiled. Connie took the key and opened the trunk. There was a blanket, and under the blank were stacks of money. Connie jumped and shivered. Mr. Braden, what the hell is this?

"A group of people thought you needed a getaway fund."

"A little more explanation, if you please." Connie covered the money, walked to Nicky, and held his hands.

"Sometimes in the underworld, people spend a long time building an escape or getaway fund, so if things break down, they can disappear.

Since you were dropped into a world surrounded by such people, it was decided that you needed such a fund. Just in case."

"What's the just in case?"

"Who knows."

"So, this is so we can ride off into the sunset if the cops are coming over the ridge." Connie still sought to wrap her head around the gesture.

"No. This fund is yours and the baby. One day, you may need to escape all this, including me, and never look back. Alimony and child support won't be an option."

"Nicky, for the first time, you are scaring the hell out of me."

"Good because they taught us in the Marines that a good dose of fear is good. It reminds you that you are not invincible. That you don't always know what's around the next corner. And that you need to complete certain tasks and make your way to a safe place. You need to take this money. It is not clean, so you cannot deposit it in a bank. Hide it somewhere no one, even me, would find it in a million years, and pray every night you never need to use it."

"Nicky, is this your way of saying that once I walk down the aisle with you, there is no turning back?"

"Connie, there has been no turning back since I fell in love with you. And even if you don't take it for yourself, take it for our baby."

Connie placed Nicky's hand on her stomach. "Nicky, I know who and what you are. I know who and what your sister and that bratty little Libby are. I have made my choice, and it is to stay with you. So, if anyone or anything threatens to stop you from coming home to me and the baby, do whatever you must to stop them first." Connie stared into Nicky's eyes, assuring she had his fullest attention. "And promise me you will try to never leave us?"

"Oh, Connie, I promise." And he kissed her.

"By the way, the doctor is doing some test tomorrow, and she wants to know if we want to know the sex of the baby."

"Gender won't change the love we put into this child, so it's up to you."

"I want to know so people can stop saying it. I am having a baby, not an it."

Nicky smiled, trying to remember if he had used the term himself.

Chapter 32

Finally, the day of the wedding came. They had been blessed with a beautiful day, and the minister decided to move the wedding outside and marry the couple on the steps of the Church. This was prudent since the crowd exceeded the five hundred expected. Several known politicians, federal movers, and shakers were in attendance, with large bodies of photographers and news persons. Libby hung on the arm of Alonso as her strutted her around, introducing her as his brother's daughter who had come to keep an eye on him in his later years. Libby noticed that one of the bodyguards that had picked her up on the night she met Alonso seemed to be trailing her. While Alonso was discussing banking with one of the local bankers, Libby approached the bodyguard.

"Is there a problem, Ms. Pettibone?"

"No. Being a bodyguard for all those years, I am not used to someone watching over me." She smiled.

"My name is Dooley. If there is anything you need, no matter how big or small. No matter if it's legal or illegal, see me first." The broad, stern face of Dooley attempted his version of returning a smile. Dooley was a large man with an old-world Irish accent and hands like catcher's mitts.

"Thank you, Dooley, and I will try not to be as stupid as some of the people I have had to watch over."

Dooley came even closer to a real smile. "Ms. Pettibone, do you mind if I ask you a question?"

The crowd in front of the First Baptist Church in Sexton, Missouri, grew. The caterers rushed about like marines on maneuvers.

"Only if you agree to call me Libby when no one else is around."

"Deal. Libby, I understand you worked for Savannah Janus. She has a lot of female bodyguards. She says it's because when she squats to take a leak, she wants a woman there to cover her ass, not some guy. Would you prefer we get a woman here to watch over you when necessary?"

Libby entertained the thought for a second before responding. "You can add a woman for times when appearance is important. But we both know there are times when there is no substitute for good old-fashioned mussel."

Dooley's eyes widen as if Libby had spoken in the secret code of bodyguards or breached their special language. He now knew. Yes, Libby was one of the fold and would be protected at all costs.

HOLLEY WORKED TO HELP Connie into her gown, fastening the buttons in the back. "They had to let it out twice since they started the fittings. This baby bump is growing faster than planned. The dressmaker asked if I wanted something in front to conceal it. I told her hell no. I have never been prouder of anything in my life."

"It's beautiful. And you are beautiful. I always dreamed of the day when I would be helping a daughter prepare for a wedding. I guess I never thought it would be these circumstances."

"Whatever the circumstances, I am so glad you are here. Is Nicky as nervous as I am?"

"It has always been hard to tell when Nicky is nervous." Holley stood back to admire the beauty that Connie projected on this day.

There was a light tapping on the door, and when Holley peaked out, there was Adam, Nicky's boss at the law firm. Adam was carrying two jewelry boxes.

"May I have a moment allow with the bride?"

"It would only seem fitting," Holley answered, leaving the two alone for the moment.

Adam stood transfixed, staring at Connie's baby bump. Connie took his hand and placed it on the bump. "It's sort of a tradition," Connie assured Adam.

"So is this." Adam opened one of the boxes and took out a diamond necklace surrounded by rubies and set in gold.

"Oh God, Adam, you want me to wear that it must cost a fortune."

"I had one made for both my daughters when they wed. I only feel it fair that this one is for Nicky's bride. It's yours, my dear. The other box is the one that was made for Cole when the time comes. In case I am not around, I want you to be the keeper."

"Tell me something, Adam. Joining me and Nicky was your plan all along, wasn't it?"

"You only ask because you did not know Nicky before the two of you met. I saw the change that quelled his heart. Did you know his mother killed his father, and Nicky was like brother and father to Cole when they were young?"

"I know they have a special bond, and I will do everything I can not to change that. Besides, I really like her."

Adam prepared his retreat, and Connie stopped him. "Do you know why no one will tell me where my honeymoon is going to be?"

"But of course. But being a lawyer by trade, I know when to keep my mouth shut. I will return to walk you down the else."

The guests for the wedding assembled for the ceremony. There were gangsters and their bodyguards from all over the world.

There was an army of federal authorities and political officials. News cameras and print reporters flocked to catch even the smallest of unique details. The event went smoothly. No one felt the need to misbehave. Cole caught the bridal bouquet, and Matt, her boyfriend, winked at her.

Chapter 33

Two girls, one about nine and the other a teenager, ran with two small Labrador puppies to meet Nicky and Cole as they stepped from the limo. They had finally arrived at their destination. It had taken a private plane to Sarasota, then a different private aircraft to the undisclosed island, where they landed on a private airstrip.

"Uncle Nicky." The two girls screamed in unison.

"These young ladies are Clair and Brenda." Nicky introduced, and he insisted his new bride from the limo.

"Where is Cole?" Clair, the younger of the two, asked.

"A gentleman does not take his sister on his honeymoon." A stern, commanding voice noted as a man in his late sixties walked up. He was dressed casually in beach shorts with a matching shirt and sandals. But even so casually dressed, his appearance commanded respect. A thin blonde woman of the same age group ran up as if the group had left her in their excitement. She was beautiful despite the appearance of the lines of time that defined her face. She wore a thin beach smock over her one-piece suit.

"Connie, this is Dominic and Estell. Our host."

Estell rushed up to hug Connie. "We have set up the guest bungalow for you two, so you will have your privacy." Estell released Connie, then stood staring at her again, then hugged Connie even tighter. Estell was similar to Connie because she did not come from a crime family.

Estell had been a schoolteacher.

Her husband was killed in a mistaken identity case by men working for Dominic. Dominic and Estell met at her husband's funeral, and a bond formed that later bloomed into love. Estell had adopted Clair and Brenda, whose parents had been killed in the same unfortunate mishap.

"Needless to say, my wife is happy to see you have found a good wife. And I am happy to see you find a little peace. I heard a little about those illegal organ harvesters slaughtering all those children. What type of sick bastards chop babies up and auction off the parts?" Dominic spoke to Nicky, and a cold shiver ran up Connie's spine.

Dominic quickly understood his mistake and stopped the inquiry for the time being.

"WHAT DO YOU SUPPOSE those two are talking about?" Connie asked Estell. The group had finished dinner and sat at the beach, watching the sun go down. Nicky and Dominic sat discussing issues, and Estell joined Connie after ensuring the children were doing their homework.

"Probably the same thing they talk about every time Nicky shows up. Dominic thinks Nicky is too smart to still take chances in the streets. Protection or not, some smart ass may pop a cap in his ass. Or some cop or fed sets him up." Connie was surprised at the candor of Estell.

"So why do you think he doesn't take an administrative position?"

"Because someone else would have to watch Coles back. And that can take some doing. How do you get along with Cole?"

"Well, the truth is it was a rough start, but we get along well now. She seems to like me and understands I do not threaten the relationship between her and her brother."

"Good. He needs her just as much as she needs him, even though he doesn't show it the same way she does."

The women stared into the glowing of the sun, and it seemed to sink into the ocean in the distance. A warm breeze blew and was caused by the ball of fire descending into the vast body of cooling water. And if there is a paradise on earth, it had revealed itself.

"Have you picked a name for the baby?"

"I know what I like. We know it's a boy, and I want to name him Nicolas after his father. I thought he should have his own middle name."

"Because then he would have the choice whether or not to use the same name as his father." Estell surmised.

"That's where it gets tricky. See, I never had a good relationship with my father, nor did Nicky, so I want to give him two middle names after the men my husband respects. Nicolas Dominic Adam Braden."

Estell smiled. "Sounds like a future president to me."

"I don't think Adam would mind. Do you think Dominic would?"

"I know that man better than anyone on this planet, and I know he would love the idea."

Both women sat and watched the men for a while, unable to hear their conversation.

Finally, Estell spoke. "You know, Connie, we have a lot in common." Connie looked at Estell and reviewed her thoughts just in case Estell had been reading them. "I was not born into this life. I am a simple retired schoolteacher."

Connie shifted position, knowing whatever Estell was going to tell her was part of the reason for her honeymooning here.

"I fell in love with a man. And somehow, it fitted me into his world. The strangest thing is that most of the people that I have met have been like you. Warm, friendly people who love life and live and joke about the old days. As the days pass, I find people who judge us as the ones who are most often out of line." Estell explained.

"Funny, I have been having a lot of thoughts along that line lately."

"Don't be mistaken; our people can be harsh and rough. They kill when they feel they must. They won't wait years and spend millions of dollars on someone they know screwed up. But what they want and need most from us is to provide them a safe haven in our hearts." Estell watched the last glow of the sunset. "Do you feel you can do this for Nicky?"

"I think I already am."

"Then that's what matters most. Come, let's give the boys the good news about the baby's name."

Chapter 34

The Hammond Inn in Sexton, Missouri, is a high-end Hotel built initially for one of the known hotel chains in the 1980s when Sexton was experiencing an unprecedented growth spirt. It was built to resemble a European Chalet. The company representing the chain abandoned the project, and a local family bought the Hammond and operated it with mostly friends and family as employees. In Holley's younger days, she had made jokes with friends about someday spending the night in the Hammond. Now Holley sat in the restaurant inside the Hammond across from Alonso, unable to remember what she had ordered. They were intentionally avoiding eye contact with each other. The meeting was a final reckoning of the wedding that had gone off without a hitch.

Neither wanted to say the words final meeting and needed to figure out how to breach the subject, but finally, Alonso spoke.

"I like this place. This is my first time in a place where everyone looks like they came from the same family."

"They did; it's a family business. It's common here. Farms, car repair, you name it, most kids stay close to home and take over the family business and property."

"I thought this part of America was extinct."

Holley fiddled with her dinner, not looking up at Alonso. "Look at us like two love-struck school teenagers from feuding families," Holley commented.

"My concern is that I may lose you as a friend."

"You mean if we don't take it to the next level?" Holley questioned.

"No. I mean, you still love and worship your late husband. I have been painfully aware that I have never emotionally gotten over my wife's loss or my children's abandonment. Face it, the best we could hope for is great friendship and consultation. It's the lonely days we have most in common."

"What about sex and the physical sharing, Mr. Pettibone?"

Alonso smiled and stroked his greying hair. "Yes, this I desire, but not as a condition to be your friend."

"Alonso, I have desired it since you sat across from me and let me make fun of you the first time we met."

The two busted into a round of teenage giggles. "People have died for less."

"What if it's my choice? Can we go to your room and enjoy each other?" Holley asked.

"Only if, you are sure. I coerce people so often that maybe I no longer know when I am doing it."

"Well, then, let me make it clear. Alonso Pettibone, I want us to go to your room and make love. Now, you may have to take it slow. It's been quite a long time for me, but it is what I want."

Alonso looked around, and it took a while for him to locate the waiter. "I guess that is the one disadvantage in a small town."

"Yeah, people don't jump when you snap your fingers, here do they, mister?"

SOMETIME DURING THE night, Holley awakened and walked to the double doors leading to the balcony of the best room in the Hammond Inn. She was still emotionally intoxicated from the reeling of sex after a long time. Alonso had held her so close after their lovemaking. She seemed to absorb some of his strength. Now, she struggled to think what this all meant. Holley felt Alonso's warm hands caress her back. She had not noticed him get out of the bed, but there he was, standing closely behind her and again in full erection. Holley turned to embrace him, and there was a shot. Not a pistol. But a riffle. Something people raised around farms knew. Then, a series of shots. Her back was burning, and she grabbed for Alonso. Holley could feel Alonso gasping for air. She now realized she was lying naked on top of him on the floor. She struggled to realize what had happened, but only darkness came to her.

Chapter 35

Nicky and Connie lye sleeping in a double hammock on the bungalow's porch.

Nicky and Connie both woke to the angry screaming Dominic coming from the main house. Nicky jumped up and ran for the main house with Connie on his heels.

"Who would do such a thing," Dominic screamed, throwing the satellite phone across the room. "Some one-shot Alonso and his girlfriend."

"Calm down, honey. Nicky is here. He will investigate it. Won't you, Nicky?" Estell asked.

"Nicky, everyone knows Alonso is no great kingpin these days. Mostly, he carries messages from me to the families. If someone thinks they can stop or reverse a message from me by slaughtering him, they are out of their fucking minds. I will burn their houses down." Dominic ranted.

"Should I leave?" Connie asked, not sure she noticed she was still in the room.

"No," Estell answered. "The woman in his hotel room was Holley Braden. Looks like this is as close to family business as it gets."

Nicky stood there shocked, trying to regroup his thoughts like a prize fighter hit with a knockout punch in the middle of the ring. Connie wrapped herself around her new husband, knowing the sexual relationship between Alonso and Holley was news.

"Alright, Nicky now hear this. Both Alonso and your aunt are in critical condition. There is a plan fueling to take you there. Find out which family wants to be wiped off the map. They are in a hospital in that Podunk town in Missouri where you come from."

"Wait," Connie said, and everyone stopped and looked at her. "If they planned to kill Alonso, wouldn't they do it in his hometown or on their turf?"

Everyone in the room knew Connie's question had merit. They had all been so close to the forest they had missed the individual trees.

"She is right. This may be an attempt to get you back in the US." Nicky observed.

"That means the feds or local law may be involved or even actually pulled the trigger," Estell commented.

"Looks like we married the two smartest women on the planet." Dominic surmised.

"I will call my sister and Libby to get the hospitals fully covered," Nicky announced.

"Nicky, until Alonso is on his feet or until further notice, that niece is now Queen of the Pettibone family. Anybody got a problem with that; they can come see me."

CONNIE SAT DOWN AFTER returning from the small restroom on the private jet, wiping her face and waiting for her pallor to return. "Flying wasn't made for pregnancy."

"Sir." The co-pilot addressed Nicky.

"Yes."

"Well, I don't mean to alarm you, but there are two Navy Interceptors, one on each side of us, and they are demanding we switch heading and not land at Pensacola International Airport."

"This is a plane, so it has to land. Where are they suggesting?"

"NAS Pensacola. The Naval Air Base. And sir, those fighters are armed, and we are not."

"Then let's hope the Navy is serving lunch."

"Never a dull day with you, is it Mr. Braden," Connie commented before rushing back to the restroom to continue her throwing up as the jet veered sharply.

NICKY AND COLE SAT in one of the officer's offices. A young female in uniform did what she could to make Connie comfortable, but there were limits, under the circumstances. The Pensacola temperature was humid, and the accommodations paled compared to the island they had left.

"Gee. Agent Winchester, this seems like a lot of trouble to cop a feel, don't you think?"

Nicky commented as Agent Winchester of the FBI led two men into the room.

"Keep your perverted fantasies to yourself, Braden." Winchester retorted. "This is Special Agent McLaughlin, assistant director of the FBI and Detective Freemont of the organized crimes task force."

"This is Connie, my wife and the woman your ring modeled for."

"Have your hands always been so manly?" Connie asked.

"Look, we need to get you two back to your planned destination to visit your folks at the hospital, but we need to ask a couple of questions first."

"Are the people you deal with always so dramatic?" Connie asked Nicky.

"Pretty much."

"Do you and Dominic know who made the move?" Freemont, a muscular man in a worn suit, asked.

"You guys are cops, and we just lost the last two days of our honeymoon. Maybe you could tell us." Connie snapped.

"I was at the wedding, and all the families seemed to be playing extremely nice. Joking about the old days and telling tales of the disappointment so many of their kids and grandkids turned out to be. Then this." Mclaughlin, a preppy-looking man slightly older than Nicky, outlined.

"Do you think it had anything to do with your ex-girlfriend's decapitation?" Freemont asked.

"Decapitation?" Connie shrieked.

"Yeah, that's where we find the body, but no clue as to where her missing head might be." Freemont defined. Connie gave Nicky a sharp look.

"It's news to me too. I thought she was somewhere sulking." Nicky concluded.

"Who moves up in the Pettibone family?" McLaughlin asked.

"Honeymoon," Nicky commented.

Winchester kept staring at Connie. "I read somewhere that you were married before. Did your ex-husband somehow accidently lose his head too?"

Connie's hormones started kicking in, and she responded to Winchester. "No, my ex-husband is afraid of my new husband. He is hiding under a bed or something, but if he shows up, I will give him your phone number and tell him you are interested in giving head."

All the men in the room chucked.

"What caliber was the bullet?" Nicky asked.

"308," Winchester answered.

"What distance?"

"Slightly less than 100 yards."

"Was the round standard or hand packed?"

"Standard right off the shelf." Winchesters face contorted trying to guess what direction Nicky was headed.

"How many guards did Alonso have at the motel?"

"Two. Long time guys." Now, the next question is mine. Any chance that niece that had no real birth records until recently has something to do with this." Winchester asked.

"I can answer that one. No way she adores both." Connie protested.

"I want to let you know you are walking a thin line between your buddies in the mob and the law. Screw up, and even we may not be able to save you. Any questions?" McLaughlin asked.

"Do you guys serve a tuna salad sandwich somewhere around her?" Connie asked.

Chapter 36

"How long have your aunt and uncle been married, ma'am?" The detective at the hospital, taking the information down on his notepad, asked.

"They aren't married. And she is my aunt, and he is her uncle." Cole added, nodding at Libby, who stood there with Matt.

"Then they both have spouses?" The detective asked.

"They are both widowed," Matt answered, straining to move the questions along, knowing how short-tempered his girlfriend could be at times like these.

"How often do they have a date night? The hotel was booked for a week."

Cole looked at Matt and asked. "Is this guy really this stupid? He couldn't find his way out of a phone booth."

Matt gestured the detective to the side to try and fill in the blanks.

Dooley walked into the room with an even more the usual somber look on his face. "May we talk privately, Ms. Pettibone."

"I failed you, and I am not proud of that fact. He may die, and it's all my fault." Dooley tried to explain when he and Libby were alone in the hallway.

"How is that?"

"They planned to meet, have dinner, and talk like they always do. The romantic interlude was spontaneous; she was such a classy lady. And we had no way to change the protection."

"Look, Dooley, he isn't dead yet. And I know how hard it is to plan protection if the package makes a last-minute change."

"There is more Ms. Pettibone."

"Libby, when we are alone, call me Libby, remember."

"No, ma'am, not anymore. As per Dominic, you are now acting Queen of the Pettibone family as of this morning. Everything now goes through you."

The news almost caused Libby to drop to the floor. She wanted to press a slowdown button, but there was none.

"They say the doctors wants to talk to us now." Matt came into the hall, not sure what he had interrupted.

"Well, it looks like your aunt will live. The key bullet went through her scapula and out her chest wall. Since the two were in an embrace at the time, the same bullet entered his chest and is causing us the problem. I need you to all be prepared for him not to survive."

The doctor had them seated in a small office that smelled of cleaning solutions and human inner workings.

Libby dropped her head in her lap, and Cole touched her back. "Nicky and Connie will be here soon."

"I need to see him," Libby said, standing.

"Are you sure?" The doctor asked.

"She's sure," Cole confirmed.

LIBBY HELD ALONSO'S hand with Cole, allowing them a private moment watching from the doorway. Alonso had a tube in his nose and was attached to a group of machines that clicked and buzzed. "I am going to make you proud of me. I will wear your name with pride. There is no way I will disrespect my new family. If you see Franco, tell him I still love him more than anyone I have ever known." Libby whispered. An alarm went off, and people started calling code blue. Slowing, Libby walked to Cole. She knew Alonso had simply been waiting for her to say goodbye. Now, he was gone. "Let's go see Aunt Holley together." Libby requested to Cole, and they walked past the teams of medical professionals on a futile mission to save a man who was now lost to this world.

"Not one of you had better give me a dirty look." Holley began. "How is Alonso?"

"He didn't make it," Libby answered. Libby, Cole, and Matt surrounded the bed of Holley. She looked weak and pale.

"Such a beautiful man." Holley squeezed Libby's hand.

"Dominic says I am Queen for the time being, whatever that means." Libby tried to divert the tide on bleak emotion.

"Do the police have any Idea who shot us?"

"No, but Nicky is on his way back. He said he had to stop and find a tuna fish sandwich for Connie. Whatever that means."

"It's a good thing. But no sushi for her."

"We got to get you out of here so you can start Aunt training," Cole announced.

Chapter 37

"Remember when we talked, and we talked about what assholes some of the cunts we have to guard can be?" Dooley sat in the back of the limo with Libby. Libby had told him it was her responsibility to confront Alonso's sons.

They sat outside the penitentiary gate.

"Yeah."

"So now you are Queen. You may be required to be the biggest cunt on the planet. Lives will depend on it. You were the guard for Savannah. Think, how would Savannah act?" Dooley's tone was stern, and she respected it. "I believe in you because you grew up rough. Those third and fourth-generation rich pussies don't have a clue what it is to have to face down tough times. I did as you said and set the meeting kneecap to kneecap, no safety glass between you, so he doesn't think you are showing strength because you have a safety net."

Libby had dressed in a women's Armani business suit. She wore Alonso's signature ring around her neck on a gold chain.

She strengthened her lapels, got out of the limo, and then looked back. "Thank you for believing in me, Dooley."

IN NO WAY DID THIS version of Butler Pettibone, Alonso's oldest son, resemble even in the slightest Alonso or Franco. He was large and thick around the middle with a dullard's face. The guards led Butler into a room with tables so the visitors could visit their loved ones.

The guards remained but kept their distance so as not to eavesdrop.

"Why don't you make this meeting worth my while and unbutton the first three buttons on your blouse." Were the first words from Butler's mouth.

Libby interlaced her fingers and led forward and stared directly into the eyes of Butler. "Look, you worthless cocksucker. I represent the family, so if you don't want to show me respect, why don't I get up and walk out of here? I can make a deal with the brothers in here to give your sorry ass three beatings a day. And about that cock sucking thing, I hear the homeboys love white mouth."

"Look, a rumor was that you were a mutt. Something found in the streets."

"I am your cousin, and your father died in front of me and your uncle died in my arms. Are we still taking?"

"Yeah." He shrugged his shoulders and slumped in his chair.

"Then represent yourself like a Pettibone. Sit up and apologize for fucking up so we can talk like two civilized people."

He sat up "Sorry."

"Sorry, what?"

"Sorry cousin, Libby."

"This is the way I see your future. Option one. I can arrange for that Public Defender to be fired and get you a real lawyer. The new lawyer gets you a shrink who says you have anger management issues and must be treated."

"Won't they still keep me in here to treat me?"

"If this was a federal facility, yes. But this place is privately run. It's a business. When they see your shrink bills are bankrupting the place, they will want you out of here without discussing why."

"Then when you get out, we get you a job where you can simply report in don't do any work, and I arrange an allowance to cover the shortfall. If you do what I say the way I say, I will arrange a hooker from time to time. This is going to be important because your days of going to pick-up places are behind you since you kill mother fuckers on the dance floor."

"Allowance, don't I inherit an equal share of my father's estate."

"Wrong. He signed everything over to me. Your hairy little testicles are in my hands."

For the first time in the conversation, Butler looks horrified.

"So, I come to work for the family someday when I get out?"

"No way. If you get out of here, you will be on paper. Parole up the yen yang. You even look at another ex-convict, and they can violate you. Of course, they won't violate you right off. The cops would see you as a good target to pimp for a snitch. Only when they realize you are too freaking stupid to make a good snitch. They will set up to go down, covering one of their good snitches. At best, you last on the streets about 24 hours. Then you do a double jackknife into a pine box."

"You said there was a second option."

"Yes. You do the rest of your time here fighting off gang rape. One day, they let you out, and you spend your nights jacking off in a dark, rusted trailer, thinking about how, for work, you wear a paper hat and say do you want fries with that all day."

Butler stared at Libby for a while, and Libby stared back. She clearly won the staring contest. "God, you're no mutt. I don't know who your mom is, but you sound just like Uncle Franco."

"I need to get out of here. This place smells like unwashed men's butt cracks. Make a choice." She stood straightening out her suit.

"We do it your way."

"Good read one book a week and send me a book report."

"Why."

"Because your conversational skills are weak, it will help you focus."

"THAT PART WAS EASIER than I thought it would be." Libby confessed to Dooley as she rested in the back of the limo.

"You think he will work out."

"Not at all. He killed a guy in the middle of a dance floor over some slut he didn't even know. Then he tells his father I don't need your help and gets the dumbest legal aid lawyer he can. The kid is a career fuck up. But I must extend the offer just in case."

"Spoken like a true Pettibone," Dooley commented.

"Dooley, I am staying at the mansion tonight. Get me a hooker."

"Any special preference?"

"Yeah. See if they have a quiet one."

Chapter 38

"Nicky, do you remember the day you came to live with me?" Nicky stood by a window in Holley's hospital room. Night had fallen, and he had asked to be alone with her.

He stood there quietly, listening to the beeps and clicks of the hospital machines surrounding her as she lay in bed.

"Yes." He finally answered.

'I remember that you wanted to bring your sister there to be safe from herself. But I saw more. I saw that you had been forced to fill in the gaps your parents made in your lives."

Still, Nicky watched the street, lost in thought and seeing something he thought should not be there.

"You were forced from your childhood to care for and protect others. Sometimes from themselves. A grown man before your time. But Nicky, I am a grown woman and don't plan on explaining myself to you or anyone else."

Nicky turned to look at her and then spoke. "Holley, I love you. I feel you love me. I don't think that the woman you are would recklessly lie down with a man without having feelings for him. I am so sorry for your pain." Nicky could not completely see Halley's face in the shadowy light, but it did not matter. He knew her well enough to know every facial expression that matched the tones in her voice.

"He was such a sweet man. I believe most of his nefarious days were behind him."

"Because of you?" Nicky asked.

"No, because of Libby. She was the link to the brother he had lost and felt guilty for not going to see when he was dying."

"How long had the two of you been intimate." Nicky strained to ask the questions he knew he needed to for his investigation.

"He had asked me to his room on several occasions. On this night, I ask him. It was our first night as more than friends."

"Did anything you can remember seem out of place about the night?"

"No, it would have been perfect. I think he loved me. I know it's odd to say, but a part of him fell in love with me the first night we met."

"There are police and federal agents that may wish to talk to you. Adam will have someone available to be with you for any questions they may have."

"My turn for a question. Everyone kept referring to you and Cole as my children at the wedding. I have never been prouder in my life." She paused for the real question. "Is Savannah's child yours?"

"No. She wants it to be unclear who the father is for her own reasons. And for the record, you have been more a mother to us than our own mother ever had the capacity to be."

Nicky went back to staring out of the window, and Holley lay back on the bed, each unable to fully see each other but enjoying the company of the other all the same.

Chapter 39

"Ms. Pettibone is not yet up, Mr. Braden," Dooley stated as he came to the estate. Nicky had noticed unmarked police cars following him, but this was normal. "She had a late night."

"You mean he had company last night?" Nicky assessed.

"I think she needed someone for the moment."

"We have all been there, Dooley. May I ask you some questions about the night Alonso got killed?"

"Sure. Does Dominic see it as my fault? Is he planning to have me hit?"

"Right now, we are in the, what happened and where does this leave up part of things."

"So, ask away."

"Do you recall anything strange about the night?"

Dooley looked like there was something he wanted to say but needed to learn how to word it.

"Whatever it is, say it?"

"Well, sir, it's just that I love my mom, and I know Ms. Holley is like a mother to you and Cole. In some ways, she is like that to Libby, too. And Ms. Holley is a real class act. I know if some guys were to say something about my mom that I thought was even the slightest bit out of line, I would take a poke at him."

"I promise not to take a poke at you."

Dooley had been polishing the car in front of the estate when Nicky walked up. Now, it seemed like he was trying to polish a hole in one spot. "It's just that going to the room was her idea. That's what changed the security. They usually met, had dinner, and laughed. I even saw them dance once, but always a peck on the cheek and good night. A PG date."

"So, you didn't plan to have to watch as much area." Nicky filled in.

"And pardon my French, but a fucking sharpshooter pops up in Mayberry. How unlikely is that? I still can't wrap my mind around that."

"We need you to keep a close eye on Libby." Nicky did not bother to say who we were.

"I will protect her like she was my own."

"Girl or guy?"

"I beg your pardon."

"Don't be a prude, Dooley. Did Libby select a girl or guy last night?"

"Some hot chick with tattoos like she has. Gee, I think I am getting old."

Chapter 40

Nicky contacted the nest and had a list of all the rental cars in the area for the week pulled. Then he got a list of all the hotel and motels in the area. I had the nest compile a list of the credit card numbers and matched them with the faces on the driver's licenses and then had someone go to the hotels, car rental agencies, and restaurants in the area. Work that would have taken a week took only hours with the help of the nest, the computer, and the accounting team for the Law firm. Much of this was illegal, but Nicky was able to move quickly, knowing the police were using a similar method to track a killer.

Nicky had quicky identified five people in the area that were using fake licenses to rent car and or hotel rooms.

LIBBY AND COLE STOOD on a playground field watching a young couple and their child. The woman was at least eight months pregnant and had red hair and a pale complexion with freckles. It was the man, however, that most caught Libby's attention. He was slender and good-looking and the spitting image of his father.

The man was Jackson Pettibone, Alonso's second son. The playground was outside an apartment complex in Philadelphia.

Dooley and two other Pettibone bodyguards stood waiting to spring into action if called on. When Libby had made it known that she needed to go to Philadelphia to speak with Jackson, Dooley contacted the crime family that boasted this area has their own. The local crime family sent two cars of backup in the event that anyone wanted to harm Libby.

Jackson kneeled, helping his daughter fasten her jacket, and Libby and Cole walked up.

"Jackson Pettibone, you are just as I pictured you."

Jackson looked at Libby, then to Cole and then at the squad of bodyguards and spoke. "Whatever you are selling, we don't want any." His tone was bland, as if rehearsed and stated a million times in the past.

"I'm not selling anything. I am your cousin, Libby."

The red-haired woman moved in closer to hear the conversation.

"I don't have a cousin Libby, lady."

"I am." Libby stopped and swallowed. "I am Franco's daughter."

"Look, whatever you say your name is. I don't want any, and you can take the band of gangsters lurking around you out of here. We are decent folks."

"Screw him Libby you tried." Cole stated.

"And fuck you too lady." Jackson's eyes now showed anger and rage.

"Stop right there Jackson. Right now, the only one out of line is you. Using that type of language in front of Hazel." Jackson's pregnant wife scolded. She stepped close to Libby, which caused the bodyguards to shift, looking for one even remotely hostile move. "I am Beth, Jacksons wife." She introduced herself, reaching for the ring around Libby's neck.

"I know this ring." This caught Jacksons interest.

"He passed away." Libby offered.

"Bad ends to bad people, I always say." Jackson's comment not only seemed to anger Cole and Libby but Beth as well."

"Look, Jackson, Franco died in my arms. I nursed him and watched him deteriorate. Some asshole shot your father while he was in the embrace of a beautiful Christian woman. The only reason I came was because I think I owe it to you not to be like you." Libby's tone how had fire.

"What do you mean?"

"I mean, when Franco died, I would have given anything for someone from the family to come and comfort me. Even just a little. But no one came. So, screw you if you didn't get the perfect toy one Christmas, or he caught you masturbating once too often. I came as a representative of the family you belong to whether you like it or not."

It was clear from the look on Coles's face she was proud of Libby.

Beth stared at Jackson, clearly waiting for him to undo some of what he had done.

"Look, Libby, I am sorry. I was being selfish. I heard Franco had a kid somewhere, but no one told me where you were."

Libby reached over and touched Jackson's hands. "You have the same beautiful hand as your father and uncle."

"You must come and hear him play. He plays all types of piano music." Beth offered.

"Do you always travel with such heavy security?" Jackson had to ask.

"No. But her life may be in danger, and we won't let anything happen to her. By the way, my name is Cole."

"Oh, shit. I mouthed off to Nicky Braden's twin sister. I guess I am lucky to be alive." Jackson joked.

"It's early yet." Cole responded.

Chapter 41

Nicky walked across the lawn toward the California Janis estate. The estate and been built during the great days of probation and bootlegging originally. The original owner had gotten involved in the motion picture industry in the US and abroad and wanted a home as luxurious as those of the cinema stars but built where he had control over the local law enforcement agencies and local politicians. A newer and more lavish mansion had been built on the property, and the original mansion was now called the stockage. It was used to house bodyguards and had quarters for both single and married employees.

Nicky had had a perfectly dreadful flight, as if the god of flying were paying him back for all the private jet air travel he had been doing. This recent fight was commercial and had three layovers. None of which departed on time. The restaurants in the airport all had lines so long Nicky and given up on the idea that he might ever eat again. There were people that kept trying to talk to him, but he needed to think, and he tried not to appear rude. Upon his landing, his first stop was to the FBI office of Special Agent Maddox. Nicky had met Maddox on an earlier visit, and Nicky needed information before he met with Savannah Janus. The meeting with Maddox proved fruitful for both men.

Now Nicky had no longer been cleared at the Guard shack for the Janus estate when he heard the guards laughing and pointing. Nicky turned to see what they were pointing at, and it was Bebe. Bebe is the computer and accounting genesis that help Nicky figure out the heads and tails of the business affairs of many businesses. Nicky had help set Bebe up on a date with Rhino, Richard Richmond and now the two were an item. Bebe is a big woman. That is why when Nicky saw her running full seed at him, he was shocked. "Nicky."

She screamed, just prior to tackling with him and landing on top of him.

"Oh, God, Bebe, I think you broke something."

"Thank you. Thank you. Thank you." Bebe exclaimed, raining a kiss on Nicky.

"Please stop slobbering on me. And let me up."

The guard at the guard shack were now laughing so hard they had to hold each other up.

"Call me Supergirl."

"What?"

"You know I like it when you call me Supergirl."

"Bebe, Richard is a giant and if he sees us rolling around in the grass, he will kill me first."

"Then you had better say it fast."

"Alright let me up Supergirl." Nicky laughed.

"Why are you thanking me anyway?"

"Well, we were at your wedding, and Rhino turns to me and speaks. Well, babe, I think we need to set a date." She showed him her engagement ring.

"That sounds so romantic in sort of a caveman sort of way."

"That's a lot of words for Rhino."

"OH, DEAR SHE RUINED your suite. The pocket is torn, and the sleeve is ripped." Savannah commented as she greeted Nicky.

Nicky had been led into the pool house by one of the maids. He had seen her before but had no idea what her name was. Since the

California and the New York branches of the Janus family had been working closely together, much of the personnel had been reassigned. Savannah greeted Nicky, wearing a light see-through cover. "So, Braden who do you think has the better baby bump me or your new wife?"

"The race is too close to call."

"Spoked like a newlywed. Now if I can just get you to stop grab assing around with your fat friend." The room had a massage table and the chair set up for a chair massage. Savannah handed Nicky a small jar of Coco butter; he had not noticed due to her current state of undress. "Start with the neck and shoulders." Savannah commanded, removing her cover and straddling the massage chair with her back toward him.

"I am sorry you must have mistaken me for your cabana boy."

"Look, buddy, this meeting was your idea. Your last-minute idea. So, you expect me to suffer loss because you didn't plan ahead."

"Spoken like a true mob Queen."

"Don't upset me or it will make me tighter, and you will be here longer. And I know how much you dislike California."

Nicky pulled up a stool and began massaging her neck, moving his thumbs along the tendon area. Then he slowly began massaging her shoulders.

"Damn, how did I know you would be so good at this?" Savannah purred.

"What happens if Jackie Boy shows up."

"I run Jackie not the other way around, besides he is taking care of some business out of town. Seems lately the word airplane in a sentence makes us want to barf."

"What can you tell me about Detective Bobby Sharps disappearance?"

"Are you asking for you or the cops?"

"Screw the cops. They have been in the middle of this fuck up all along. A lot of good cops too loyal to see the bad ones."

"If we are being honest, your twin sister is no angel. She had an open affair with Bobby while his wife was carrying child number five, if I am not mistaken. And when he got hooked on her stuff and wanted to make her his new baby-making machine, she balked."

"You can say anything bad about her you want. I know how much you like her."

"So much so that when I found out he had shamed her in the police station, I set some usually reliable guys to pay him a visit."

"How did it go?" Nicky continued massaging her back.

"Slide your hand around and rub my tummy. They say it will help the skin stretch and prevent stretch marks. I wear a lot of bikinis, you know."

Nicky did as he was told.

"They killed a man and woman that were in the house screwing at the time and burned the place to the ground. We all thought that was the last of Detective Bobby Sharp, philandering womanizer."

"Then you found out the life insurance company refused to pay the widow because there was no conclusive match to the body. Which meant the widow might spend the next seven years staring to death while standing on the side of the road with a will work for food sign and five depressed children."

"Only a good-looking man could set such a colossal fuck up in motion. If you are here asking about him, you think he is still alive." Savannah moved his hands up to massage her breast. "Can't have stretch marks there either."

Nicky continued to massage. "I think I saw him. The other night when I was looking out of my aunt's hospital room window."

Savannah stopped the massage, then turned and faced Nicky. "How is Libby holding up?"

"A lot of people are pulling for her."

"Did you know Alonso would check up on her secretly?"

"No."

Savannah smiled. "Do you still have her fire engine red thong."

"What thong?" Nicky convincingly tried to conceal the truth.

"I seem to remember at a party, she shoved something into your jacket pocket that looked like a red thong."

"I remember the party, and I remember her putting something in my pocket for safekeeping, but I am sure it wasn't a thong."

Savannah left the room and returned in a few minutes. She handed Nicky an envelope filled with cash. "When you talk to Sharps widow, give her this. And Nicky, when you run across Sharp, be sure you kill the mother fucker."

"That's the plan."

Chapter 42

Nicky walked up the driveway to the house where Leonetta Sharp lived. There was no mistake. He had the right place.

There was what looked like a half dozen small children teasing and chasing each other as a woman holding a child too young to join the frivolity clung to her. The woman secured the child with one hand and smoked a cigarette with the other.

The infant watched the woman take long drags from the cigarette as if it was the most essential life lesson the child must know.

Leonetta Sharp was a thin, black, very light-skinned woman who, other than the dark, sleepless circles accumulating beneath her eyes, looked hardly old enough to have so many children. "What happened to your clothes?" Leonetta asked, eyeing the torn places and grass stains.

"I got tackled."

"Big guy?"

"Big girl. Old friend, glad to see me."

Leonetta smiled. "Well, you clearly aint no cop. And you aint a suck ass Fed, so come on in while I lay the baby down, and you can tell me why you are here."

All the furniture in the Sharp home had seen its better days. There was a small table near the doorway that was weighted down with past due and collection notices. There was depressing air flowing through the home and no sign of past good times or the prospect of future ones.

"First, I need to be honest with you. I am Nicky Braden; my sister was seeing your husband."

"You mean she is one of the many slutts that couldn't keep their grubby little paws off a married man."

Nicky's expression clearly showed he had no idea what to say or if anything he learned here would be of value to him.

"Did she take the money?" Leonetta asked.

"What money?"

"The morning after Bobby came up missing. I thought to be in that fire, our bank account had been drained. And he had a lock box in the garage with cash that he didn't think I knew about; it was emptied out."

"No, she didn't take your money. But that's why the feds stopped you from collecting on your insurance."

"You are saying that weasel split and left me with a house full of hungry kids. Hardly seems like something a real man would do, does it?" Leonetta lit another cigarette. The smoke blended into the other depressed odors of the room.

"A friend of my sisters wants you to have this."

Leonetta began crying as she accepted the envelope. "No strings."

"No strings," Nicky answered.

The reverse of recent misfortune took a while for Leonetta to absorb.

"Did he keep a riffle here?"

"How did you know? It's missing too."

Chapter 43

"Nicky, I liked that suit. What happened to it?" Nicky had another series of bad flights to return to the Sexton, Missouri home. He searched the refrigerator for anything edible.

"How is Aunt Holley?" He asked, not yet answering Connie's question.

"She is upstairs resting. We have a nurse coming in to visit twice a day. Now, about the suit."

Nicky found some cold fried chicken and began eating it.

"Is Matt still in the house?"

"Yes, but he is packing to leave; he has to go back to work." Connie smiled, watching devour the chicken.

"Cancel his flight. He must stay in the house, and so do you. There is some extra security showing up soon."

"Do I get to know what the problem is? And what about the suit?"

"Bebe happened to the suit; she tackled me."

Connie burst into laughter. "And you couldn't move out of the way. You two aren't kids."

"She would have fell on her face."

"What about the lockdown?"

"Short term, I got to fix a problem."

"And you need to make it home for regular meals. Now, is this where I tell you to go out and get the bad guy?"

"Well, I actually am the bad guy."

NOW, KNOWING WHAT NICKY knew, it was easy to locate Bobby. With a physical description, check the local motels with someone who checked in with a fake driver's license. He made it a point to ask the clerks about the person staying in the room where Bobby had booked. He wanted Bobby to know he was closing in. Nicky then went to the coffee shop across the street. He laid a napkin across the table in front of himself.

Nicky called Dooley. Nicky took out a small tape recorder, sat it on the table, and waited.

Nicky did not have to wait long.

"Alright, this is a stick-up; everybody put your hands up." A man in a ski mask ran into the coffee shop waving a gun.

The man turned and looked at Nicky.

Their eyes locked for a moment.

There was a lone shot. The masked man hit the ground, holding his thigh.

Nicky had shot him with a gun he had hidden beneath the napkin. Dooley turned around from the counter and removed the weapon from the masked man's hand.

"Everybody relaxes, and somebody calls the cops," Dooley instructed. Dooley pulled up the mask, and it was Bobby Sharp. Nicky took a chair and moved it close to Bobby.

"Fuck you, Braden. That was a cheap shot."

"I shot your femoral artery; you will be dead before you reach the hospital. But we might talk in the meantime."

"Sure." Bobby coughed, and blood filled his nose.

"Why did you shoot Alonso?"

Bobby tried to laugh, but it was caught in a cough that made blood form in his mouth. "That was a total screw-up on my part. You have been in the service. A shot at less than a hundred, you hit what you aim at." Bobby's eyes rolled upward as he reconciled the pain. "I thought your aunt was screwing some old dairy farmer or deacon from the church. Fuck how was I supposed to know that little old lady was fucking a crime kingpin. And the 308 passes straight through her like a hot knife through butter."

"Why."

"Because your sweet little sister cost me everything. I did some of those out-of-town hits and had a nice sum stored. You come to town, and I'm on the run."

"Nice trap, Braden. Have you ever thought about doing this stuff professionally?" Dooley joked.

"I do. And the tape will clear Dominic's ill will against you."

Dooley and Nicky sat and waited for the police while watching the death ashy grey come to Bobby's face."

Chapter 44

Nicky sat beside LeAnn, his legal representative, in the office of FBI Special Agent McLaughlin. LeAnn was Asian and small but forceful.

Agent Winchester reentered the room. "It all checks out. Maddox and the California FBI office have been looking at former Detective Bobby Sharp as part of that hitman cop thing he is working on."

"When can my client expect his medal?" LeAnn asked.

"You walk a fine line, Mr. Braden. One day, you will tip over." McLaughlin assessed.

"Why didn't you call a cop if you thought you had found the killer?" Winchester asked.

"And have the good cops or the bad cops show up. Really Ms. Winchester, did you graduate at the bottom of your class by chance?" LeAnn riddled. "My client just saved the lives of all the people in that coffee shop. The police have found the rifle that killed Alonso Pettibone and tried to kill Mrs. Braden. There is murder for hire charges that were outstanding on this man, and you people want to sweat my client. Shame on you."

COLE AND MATT SAT IN the middle of the floor in the soon-to-be nursery in the Sexton home. They were in the process of putting together a crib that came unassembled. Libby watched Carol, a nurse who had been visiting Holley. Carol and Libbby had been on a couple of dates. Carol was a chubby girl with a bubbly personality.

"Look who's walking?" Connie stated. Holley was balancing herself between Her and Nicky.

"This doesn't make any sense," Cole complained, turning the diagram upside down.

"Welcome back, Aunt Holley." Libby ran to her and gave her a big hug.

"I was a little afraid to face you." Holley confessed.

"No. I could see the good part of him, too. I was glad you could warm the coldest parts of his heart. That is something Franco talked about in some of the letters. It is hard for a man who has led a rough life to find that warmth. Franco said he found it in me."

"Matt has been asked to accept a position at the local Junior College as the information technology teacher. He wants to know what we all think." Cole threw it into the mix.

"Sounds good to me." Nicky was the first to say.

Libby added "Can you help me start an educational fund for the children of the next generation? You know, like my cousin Jackson's kids and Connie's babies."

"Hey, what's these babies bull? I agreed to one."

They all began to laugh until softly Libby said. "I can't live with the thought that some kid out there is going through want I did. They are all God's children."

"Then we can make it happen, right, little brother," Cole called out.

"Everyone knows I was born first, Cole."